Spirits after Sunset

FELINES OF FAIRYTALE FOREST

BOOK THREE

K.L. MONTGOMERY

Cover design by the author, made with images licensed through DepositPhotos.
Map created by Kadan Knapp
Paperback ISBN: 978-1-949394-83-2

Published by Mountains Wanted Publishing
P.O. Box 50
Harbeson, DE 19951
mountainswanted.com

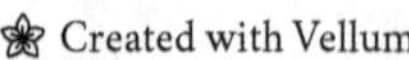 Created with Vellum

A bride in danger…or just a sick Halloween prank?

A Halloween-themed wedding is in the works at Fairytale Forest, but the custodians and cats keep finding creepy threats that reference an old Charleston ghost story. The ghost of a bride who was murdered shortly before her wedding in 1804 is said to haunt the graveyard at St. Michael's church. Is Charlotte, the Fairytale Forest bride, destined for a similar fate?

Meanwhile, Zoe's senior clowder member is missing, and other cats in the park have gotten sick. Zoe fears the worst, but she won't rest until she figures out what happened to him. Are his disappearance and the sickness somehow related to the upcoming wedding?

Can Cat, Gloria, and the Felines of Fairytale Forest follow the clues to find out who is behind the threats and sick cats? Can they prevent a third murder from happening in the park, and will they ever find out what happened to Mr. Cool Cat?

Fairytale Forest Map

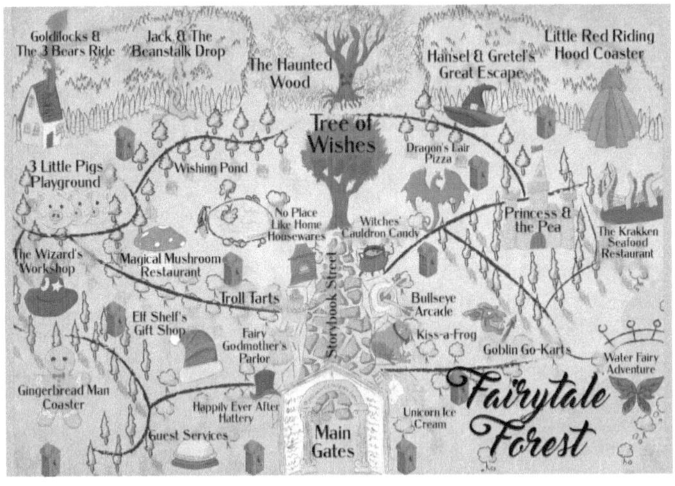

Created by Kadan Knapp

To Rebecca and Yvonne—for that wonderful night in Charleston.

Prologue

They threw down the newspaper with a scoff and turned to their companion. "Who is this Catherine Lyon? She's ruining everything! How am I going to be able to close down Fairytale Forest when she keeps interfering in my plans?"

"Is she really interfering in your plans, or just solving the murders before the public can find out about them?" the companion questioned.

Their nostrils flared as they took in the photo of Ms. Lyon and her colleague Ms. Bress shaking hands with James Forest, owner of the amusement park. They gritted their teeth. "He's giving them a week's paid vacation at his Isle of Palms beach house! Rewarding them for their help!"

"Sounds like the perfect opportunity for you to execute the next part of your plan, Master."

"Oh, I do love it when you call me that." An evil cackle spilled out of their mouth. "Mmmm…yes, and I would jump on this golden opportunity, but it's been harder to match up victims and assassins than I expected. Drat, there are too many good people with no arch enemies at that blasted park!"

"Did you see this, Master?" Their companion thrust the society section of the newspaper toward them.

"See what? Oh…" Their eyes bounced back and forth over several lines. "Ah…the best friend's daughter is getting married in the park."

They rubbed their hands together. "I am getting some ideas, Pet. Some very good ideas indeed. We can exact revenge on our foes, get the park shut down, and torment this Catherine Lyon all at the same time. That's three birds with one stone…"

One

CATHERINE

"If you would have told me a year ago that I'd be lying on the beach at Isle of Palms, basking in the sun with my bestie as the waves lap at my feet, I'd have called you crazy!" I sighed as bliss wrapped me in its warm embrace and I took another delightful sip of a frothy fruity concoction.

"In the big bosses' back yard, no less!" Gloria chimed in, raising her glass. "Here's to well-deserved rewards!"

"Well-deserved indeed!" I sipped a little too much, too fast, and experienced a momentary bout of brain freeze. But I shook it off. It would be hard to ruin my mood on this gloriously sunny October day.

"The weather is just amazing too," Gloria gestured to the sky, "the cherry on top of it all."

I sighed, adjusting my swimsuit strap. "Especially after such a grueling, oppressively hot summer. Ugh!"

"We survived, my friend," Gloria reminded me. "We

survived the weather and two murders. And now we have a whole week in paradise."

I flicked a little bit of sand off my toes and grabbed the sunblock to reapply. We'd been out here for two hours already, and I did not relish the idea of turning myself into a boiled lobster out here. Time to slather on the SPF and protect my glaringly fair skin. "I wonder how the cats are doing with us away."

"Oh, you and those cats!" Gloria giggled her sparkling laugh, brushing off my question with a hand wave. "I'm sure they are just fine, as they have been for many years now without us worrying over them."

An image of Zoe, the beautiful gray long-haired cat who had helped us solve both murders, crept into my mind. I'd been thinking about her a lot ever since we'd gotten to Isle of Palms. It was weird—and I still had no explanation for it—but I could hear her talk. And she seemed to be able to hear me as well. How? Why? I hadn't been able to figure it out. I didn't know if I should talk to an animal expert, a therapist, a psychic, or all three.

"You know, I never asked Mr. Forest how he got the idea to use feral cats to keep his park free of pests." I handed Gloria the sunblock. "Do you know? Have they been in the park the whole time you've worked there?"

"Indeed they have," Gloria answered, rubbing the lotion into the skin on her face and shoulders. "Mr. Forest's father brought the first cats into the park. They have been there longer than me. Not the same ones, of course."

"How long do they usually live?" I continued my interrogation. "What happens when one of them passes away?"

She sighed. "I don't rightly know, to tell the truth. I mean, they get old, and then they just aren't there anymore. I don't know if someone takes them away, or if they're allowed to pass naturally. That'd be a question for the Wrangler."

"They hate The Wrangler, you know."

"So you've said." Gloria laughed and adjusted her wide-brimmed straw hat. "So what do you want to get into tonight?"

"I could go for a big plate of something yummy." I rubbed my belly in anticipation. "Do you have any ideas?"

"Mrs. Forest left a list of their favorite restaurants on the desk in the kitchen. I figured we'd try one of those. If they're good enough for the Forests…"

I smiled. "Can you imagine being this rich, Gloria? Owning two mansions, one in historic Charleston and one on Isle of Palms? I just can't even fathom, ya know?"

"We've led much more modest lives." Her eyes closed as she soaked in an extra-large dose of Vitamin D. "But it's nice to see how the other half lives sometimes, isn't it?"

"It sure is," I agreed.

Before I could say anything else, a buzzing sounded from a speaker at the rear of the house. We both jerked upright in our sun loungers.

"What d'ya suppose that was?" Gloria sounded miffed that her relaxation was interrupted.

"Think it might've been the front door bell." I swung my legs over the side of the lounger. "Don't get up. I'll go see who it is."

"Wasn't planning on getting up; y'all can trust me on that, sugar!" Gloria smirked as she lowered the brim of her straw hat once more.

I ambled up the stairs to the deck, through the French doors, and zigzagged across the house to the foyer. Through the peephole, I surveyed the front porch. No one was there, but there was something on the welcome mat. A delivery? Had the Forests sent us something? They were just too kind *—first they give us the week off, allow us to use their beach home, and then they send us a gift too?*

I pushed open the door and reached down to grab the medium-sized cardboard box. It wasn't heavy—I had thought maybe it was a fruit basket. I carried it to the kitchen and grabbed a knife.

My brows drew together when they landed on a mangled bouquet of decaying flowers with a stained white bow.

I gasped when I realized the reddish-brown stains on the bow looked exactly like blood. I was a custodian, so I basically had a PhD in identifying dried bodily fluids and their corresponding cleaners.

My heart began to pound when I turned the bouquet over and noticed an attached note. I didn't even need my reading glasses to make out these two simple words:

You're next.

ZOE

"I call this meeting of the Courtyard Clowder to order," I announced as my minions began to surround me, scanning the lopsided semi-circle where they dotted the landscape.

"We need an official flag!" Ziti piped up.

"Yeah," Amber agreed, "and a pawshake!"

"A flag? A pawshake? You've been hanging out with the bipeds too much," my brother Moony scoffed.

"Excuse me," I hissed, "but this is my meeting, and I'm the one talking. Y'all shut your mousetraps now and listen up."

"Mmm, it's so hot when you talk all tough like that," Snow purred beside me.

The pure-white shorthair with the ringed tail had shown up in the park around the same time as the last dead body. It turned out he was the murder victim's owner. Well, bipeds would say the *biped* was the *feline's* owner, but we all knew differently.

To my surprise and delight, he was working out quite well, becoming one of us, assimilating into our little klatch here in the park. And he was quite complimentary of me and my leadership style. So I was pretty sure I was going to keep him. At least for the time being.

"As I was saying," I returned my attention to the assembly of fine-looking felines, "I've called the meeting to order, and tonight's first order of business is..." I scanned the crowd again. "Wait. Where's Cool?"

A low murmur arose as feline eyes shifted right and left, searching the gathered cats for our most senior member, Mr. Cool Cat. He'd been around longer than any of us. His memory had been a bit off lately, and I was concerned about him. He also seemed to be slowing down.

"Well, where is he? Has anyone seen him? Who was supposed to be watching him?" We'd divvied up Cool-sitting responsibilities, and someone had dropped the ball of yarn.

"Who?" Daisy looked around, blinking her huge amber eyes. She was a ditzy long-haired calico, and she probably didn't know her own name half the time.

"Mr. Cool Cat?" I repeated, louder this time. The murmuring instantly came to a halt. "Moony, have you seen him? Ice?" They, along with Ziti and Amber, were my most trusted, agile, and cunning hunters.

They both shook their heads.

"Anyone else? Ziti? Hank? Amber? Priss? Sass?"

"I haven't seen him since last night," Sass said, sharpening her claws on a tree root that jutted out of the ground.

"Has anyone seen him since then?" I scoured the crowd for any sign someone had information on our beloved seniormost feline.

"I wouldn't be surprised if Scar has something to do with his disappearance," Snow interjected.

I whipped my head toward him. "What makes you say that?"

"Well, isn't Scar the source of all bad things in the park?" He licked his lips and gave the feline equivalent of a smirk.

"Well, yes, but…what would he want with Cool?"

Snow lifted his shoulders slightly. "Beats me. But I still think it's a good theory."

"That's it. Meeting adjourned. We're all looking for Cool tonight." I started to walk away, frustrated by this turn of events. I knew I should have been keeping an eye on him myself, but I'd been pretty busy. *Good help is hard to find*, I lamented.

"Can we still eat?" Hank was always more concerned about food than anything else, as evidenced by his bulging belly.

"Yes, you can still eat. But look for Cool," I instructed. "That's your primary objective."

"Primary objective…you're making me…frisky." Snow rubbed up against me, and I shot him a death glare.

"Your primary objective is helping me find Cool," I hissed low enough that only he could hear. Then, to the rest of the clowder, I directed, "Go on, everyone. Get moving. Report back here at dawn."

I looked off into the distance where the pathways criss-crossing the park were lit with tall streetlamps. The side-walks were slightly shiny from a late afternoon shower. The temperatures were getting cooler. Fall had arrived in Fairy-tale Forest. I hoped Cool was safe and warm…and alive.

Two

Look! They've got the Halloween decorations up." Gloria pointed at a jack-o-lantern big enough that we could both fit inside it as we headed toward the facility services building to clock in and get our assignments and carts for our night shift.

I surveyed the boughs of vibrantly colored fall leaves that arched over Storybook Street and the matching garlands that twisted around each streetlamp. "Oh, they're very colorful this year! Last year they were so dark and kind of morbid, remember?"

"I noticed that too. I like this look—it's a little more family-friendly." Gloria nodded in approval at a huge black cat figure staked on one side of the courtyard entrance. On the other was a gigantic skeleton that waved at the passing crowds.

"That cat looks like Sass!" I noted as we headed to the building.

Gloria just sighed. "You and those cats!"

"I missed them while we were gone last week. Hopefully I'll see Zoe tonight so we can catch up." I was starting to feel pretty attached to my new feline friends.

"Yeah, and hopefully she didn't find any bodies in our absence." My colleague rolled her eyes as I swung open the door to the facility services building for her.

"Hey," our new boss, Sheri, greeted us. "Go clock in and come right back here. I need to talk to you both."

A jolt of panic raced down my spine as Gloria clutched my elbow and shot me a worried look. I smiled and nodded at Sheri. "No prob, Boss! Where's Karen tonight?"

"You're awfully chipper tonight," Sheri pointed out. "Must be that relaxing week you had on the beach. Karen is over on the other side of the park, managing a special project this week. You guys are stuck with me for a few hours."

"Hey, that week off certainly didn't hurt," I agreed as we both shuffled into the lounge and grabbed our timecards out of the metal racks before punching them in the antiquated system. The Forests were of the "if it ain't broke, don't fix it" mindset, and that applied to most of the technology in the parks.

Except for the security tech, which they were rapidly upgrading in the wake of two employee deaths. One murder was carried out by a fellow park employee, and though the other wasn't, both bodies were found on park property. Keeping the stories out of the press was a full-time job for the park's PR department. Thankfully, there was only a small article about the first death in the papers, and the second wasn't covered at all.

Mr. Forest had asked Gloria and me for help keeping it that way—by figuring out who murdered both victims as quickly as humanly possible.

Only, it took more than our human abilities to solve the mysteries.

The park's feral cat colony, charged with keeping vermin out of the park, helped, particularly one cat: Zoe.

I still hadn't decided if I was crazy or not, but Zoe and I could communicate. I could hear her speak, and she could hear me. And we understood each other. It was just the two of us. Like we had a special unexplained bond.

I had spent many hours lost in thought, wondering if I should have my head examined. Gloria was the only person who knew the cat and I could communicate. Okay, she wasn't the only person—not anymore. When we were solving the last case, Mr. Forest's son, Jayden, and Jayden's girlfriend, Nora, were helping us, and it was hard to keep it from them since Zoe played such a critical role. They promised not to tell anyone, especially not his parents.

So, every time we spoke, we had to make sure to do so in private. Zoe didn't want other humans to know she was hanging out or communicating with me because any feral cats caught getting too friendly with humans were shipped out of the park to local shelters. I'd already rescued Zoe's brother from such an incident earlier this year, and I knew she didn't want to suffer the same fate.

"Ready to go see what Sheri wants?" Gloria asked, nudging my arm. "You seem to have disappeared there for a moment."

"I'm ready, just reminiscing about our little getaway last week." I winked, and she smiled. We'd had an amazing time together at the beach.

She grabbed my arm and gave me a smile. "Come now, fren, if we take one step, God will take two." It was, no doubt, another pearl of her ancestors' wisdom, passed down through the generations and still guiding her people today— and, luckily, me too by association.

Fortified by Gloria's encouraging words, I swallowed

hard before poking my head into Sheri's office. "Hey, Boss, you wanted to see us?"

"Yes, have a seat." She gestured to the two chairs facing her desk, and we both sat down.

"What's up?" I folded my hands in my lap after I noticed Gloria had done that, and it made her appear extra prim and proper.

"Mr. and Mrs. Forest called a meeting of all the department heads earlier today," she began. "You are probably not aware, but Assistant GM Tom Carson is hosting his daughter's wedding here at the park next week. It will have a Halloween theme—you may have noticed the new decorations when you arrived at the park."

"They're beautiful!" Gloria chirped.

"Indeed. In any case, Mr. Forest told us the event is very important to him, naturally, as he and Tom go way back. They've been best friends since childhood, and Tom Sr. worked for Mr. Forest's dad here in the park. Mr. Forest's daughter, Jocelyn, is the bride's matron of honor. So the two families have a very special relationship."

I started to wonder where she was going with this. Did she just want us to keep things extra neat and tidy for the wedding? I mean, of course we would. We took great pride in our work.

"In any case," she finally continued, her dark eyes flashing as they bounced between Gloria and me, "in light of recent events, Mr. and Mrs. Forest are both worried about any further…uh…incidents occurring on the grounds that might negatively impact the wedding."

"I can understand that," Gloria agreed. "Things have been unsettling around here, haven't they?" She shivered as though there was a chill in the air, though it was still ninety degrees, even in October.

"Mr. Forest pulled me aside personally to remind me that

you were returning from your little getaway on Isle of Palms today." She ran her fingers through her short, spiky hair. "He wanted me to ask you two to be extra vigilant for signs of anything odd or out of place. He wants to get ahead of any…problems…"

Goose bumps broke out on my arms as I remembered the strange bouquet of dead flowers we received when we were staying at his home last week. I could only assume they were meant for him or his wife.

Was that a sign of an impending "problem," as Sheri just warned us about?

"Well, uh…actually," Gloria said before shifting her gaze to me and giving me a pressing look. She obviously wanted me to spill the beans.

"Now that you mention it," I took up where she left off, "we did have something kind of strange happen last week at his beach house. But, you know, we weren't in the park. And I don't know if it's even related to the park at all. Could just be a neighbor with a weird sense of humor…?"

Her lips pursed as she eyed me. "Well, are you going to tell me what happened?"

"Maybe we should tell Mr. Forest in person," I sighed, and Gloria nodded.

"Tell me first, and I'll decide if it's worth bothering Mr. Forest," Sheri said, nostrils flaring.

"Fine." I glanced over, and Gloria had moved to the edge of her seat in anticipation, her legs crossed at the ankles. "So…last week when we were at the Forests' beach house, the doorbell rang, and when I got to the door to answer it, no one was there, but I found a box on the doorstep. So I brought it inside and opened it because it didn't have a label on it or anything, and I thought maybe the Forests had sent us a gift, like a fruit basket or some other such goodies." I paused to take a breath—the words were just flying out of my mouth.

"Go on…" Sheri gestured as if to say, "give me more."

"Well, it was weird because, inside was a bouquet of dying roses and greenery, tied up with a stained white ribbon. It kind of looked like a bridal bouquet, now that I think about it, and the stains on the ribbon looked like dried blood. And there was an attached note with only two words on it."

Sheri's eyebrows flew toward the ceiling. "Which were?"

"Um…it said…" I swallowed hard, remembering how bad it creeped us out. "It said… 'You're next.'"

Our boss's eyes widened, and her lips parted as though she wanted to speak, but no words came out at first. She blinked rapidly. "And what did you do with this bouquet?"

"I left it in my car. I was going to send an email to Mr. Forest about it tonight…because I assume it was meant for him or Mrs. Forest?"

Sheri shuddered. "Don't you think that would have been an important piece of information to give him right away?"

"Well, to be honest, I put it in my trunk then forgot about it till just now. I put my suitcase in my back seat when I was leaving their place, and I haven't opened my trunk since. I'm so sorry, I—"

"Let me just give him a quick buzz. I think he's still in his office." She held up one finger and grabbed her telephone receiver with the other hand, putting it to her ear. She leaned it against her shoulder as she dialed a star and four numbers for his extension.

She reached his secretary. When she claimed she had urgent information, possibly a security issue, she was patched through to Mr. Forest immediately. She relayed my story in one breath, her eyes darting around the room nervously before they landed on me. We all held our breaths while we waited for his direction.

She hung up the phone and stared at me. "Go get the box with the flowers. He wants to see it. Then go directly to his office in the guest services building."

Gloria and I both stood up. "Should I go with her?" Gloria questioned.

"Yes. Both of you. Hurry."

THE SECRETARY SHOT US A DISAPPROVING GLARE AS GLORIA and I stood in the waiting area holding the nondescript cardboard box that was about eighteen inches long, twelve inches wide and maybe eight inches deep. It barely weighed anything at all. Finally, she wordlessly gestured for us to enter the big boss's office.

"Come on in, ladies," Mr. Forest's booming voice greeted us as he gestured us forward.

We both headed in with the reverence one might show toward their priest or minister. I gingerly set the box on the edge of his desk. "Uh…I'm so sorry we didn't tell you about this showing up at your beach house. We were just having such an amazing time, I stuck this in my trunk and forgot all about it. We're ever so grateful for the lovely stay."

"It was one of the best weeks of my life," Gloria added as Mr. Forest pointed to the chairs in front of his desk.

So, we went from sitting in Sheri's hot seats to Mr. Forest's. These were much nicer, plusher, though.

"Should I take a peek?" He scooted the box toward him as he sat back down in his luxurious leather executive chair.

"I figured it was just a sick joke." I drummed my fingers on the desk just once as he opened the cardboard flaps and pulled out the bouquet. "As you can see, there's no label on the box, and the only thing on the note is—"

He gripped it between his thumb and index finger and read aloud, "'You're next'? What in the Sam Hill does that mean?"

"I have no idea, sir." I scrubbed my hands down my face in embarrassment for not letting him know right away this had shown up on his doorstep. "Again, I'm so sorry for—"

He held a hand up to cut me off. "Please, no apologies are necessary. I'm so glad y'all enjoyed your time at the beach house. You both deserved a nice break, but I'm glad y'all are back. We're starting to prepare for Tom's daughter's wedding. Have you met Charlotte? She worked here a couple of summers ago. Of course, she was just a young'un then. Now she works as the Director of Communications at St. Michael's Church."

"Oh, that's the one with the big white tower downtown, isn't it?" Charleston was known as The Holy City for all the steeples that graced its skyline, and St. Michael's was one of its most famous and iconic buildings.

"Yes, it's the oldest church building in the city, dating back to the 1750s. George Washington once worshipped there when he was in town," he said with the gravitas expected for such a venerated figure in American history. "Anyway, Charlotte and her fiancé, Walker, are getting married in two weeks, and they have chosen a Halloween theme for their wedding. I was kinda surprised they wanted such a nontraditional wedding. I mean, why not get married in the church, you know? It's beautiful. But, anyway, they want to get married in the Haunted Wood, and it sounds like the whole ceremony will be a bit unorthodox. Tom is understandably a little nervous about it, with everything that's been going on here in the park."

"I can't say I blame him," I remarked, and Gloria nodded in agreement.

"Right, right. Well, I guess Sheri told you about the

meeting I had today with the departmental managers. I just want to hopefully head off any potential issues leading up to the big day. I promised Tom everyone would be extra vigilant. You know the whole, 'If you see something, say something' campaign, like from after 9-11?"

We both nodded. Thinking about that turbulent period in our country's history caused another crop of goose bumps to prickle my skin. Everything was so scary for a while…

"Right, well, the first people I thought of keeping an eye out for anything unusual were you two," he continued. "I trust you both have the park's best interest at heart, and you've been here long enough to know when something doesn't seem right. You're also both keen observers. So I know you will both do an excellent job surveilling the place and letting me know right away if anything at all seems amiss."

He smiled and handed us each a plastic card attached to a lanyard. "These key cards will grant you access to any door or gate in the park. I trust y'all not to abuse this access." He shot us both a wide grin. "Seriously, ladies, let me know if anything, I mean *anything* seems strange or off. Even if it seems silly. Just shoot me an email or leave me a voicemail message.

"I know you're here in the middle of the night when I'm at home with my family, but I want to know what's going on. And if it's something really serious and urgent, call me at home. Don't hesitate. Please." He took two business cards from a shiny brass holder on his desk and jotted the same phone number on both of them.

"This will go to the main house line, which is answered twenty-four-seven," he said, his lips set in a thin line. "I trust you both to know when something is urgent and when it can be relayed in an email or voicemail."

"Of course, Mr. Forest," I said. "We will both exercise our best judgment in this matter."

"As we do all matters," Gloria chimed in.

He clasped his hands together, and that thin, straight line of his lips curled up into a smile. "Thank you both so much for all you've done for me and Fairytale Forest. Hopefully, the only excitement we'll have here in the next couple of weeks is Charlotte and Walker's wedding!"

Three

ZOE

I woke up from my nap pleasantly surprised to see the sun was already beginning to set. It was so much harder to maneuver and stay hidden from bipeds when the huge yellow ball was glowing in the sky like a spotlight illuminating my every move. I noticed Moony and most of the others were still asleep, so I figured I'd take the opportunity to prowl around and see what I could see...and smell.

As a cat, I didn't have a biped concept of time like hours and minutes, but I did know bipeds were very obsessed with these things. I noted days passing, and obviously I could mark time with things like the shape of the moon and the position of the stars in the sky. Anyone who thinks animals are dumb and don't understand things like this is a fool. I knew lots of felines that were much smarter than bipeds—and the first name that came to mind as an example was Mr. Cool Cat.

He had been around the block about a million times and was probably on the last of his nine lives. He was my mentor, the closest thing I'd ever had to a father, and his presence was missed around the clowder. If he took off permanently, he didn't say goodbye, and that just didn't seem like him. That was why I suspected something had gone very wrong.

And if I found out Scar had something to do with Cool's disappearance…my wrath was going to look significantly more intense than the last two times he and his cronies crossed me.

Walking along the bushes for cover so I could make my way closer to the huge tree in the center of the park, I picked up a familiar scent: *Cat!*

My favorite biped was back.

I used to think the only valid reason for a feline to have warm and fuzzy feelings for a biped is that he or she is a reliable source of food or affection. Food was always a good bet, of course, but there were also bipeds who knew just how to scritch those hard-to-reach spots, you know? The kind that made your rear-end arch, your tail shake, and that deep purr vibrate in your throat. Cat could do that for me, naturally, but there was more to our relationship than that.

She saved my brother. And so I was forever indebted to her.

She'd grown on me like a fungus, and I had to admit, the warm and fuzzy feelings were there to stay.

Though bipeds typically associated loyalty with those drooly, nasty, butt-sniffing canines, cats could also show a great deal of loyalty to those who were deserving.

Cat was deserving.

I followed the trail until there were too many bipeds about to continue risking it, and I had to camp out and wait for the traffic to die down. Then, in a lull, I scurried across the courtyard to where her scent strengthened. It led me to the building where the cleaning bipeds hung out when they weren't working, and where they stored their huge carts full of cleaners, buckets, mops and other supplies.

Bipeds sure were obsessed with cleaning stuff. Felines were more rightly focused on keeping ourselves clean. Some bipeds could take a lesson from us in hygiene and grooming, ya know?

As I was waiting in the shadows to see if she would come out of the building, I saw something shiny near the entrance. It appeared to be a thin silver chain hanging from a branch of a bush growing next to the steps up to the building. An oval-shaped metallic object dangled from the chain.

It was pretty and shiny, and I thought maybe Cat might like to have it. I could give it to her as a welcome-back-to-work present because, even though I wasn't sure exactly how long she had been gone, I did know she and her buddy Gloria had missed several consecutive days, more than usual. She said something about "going to the beach for a week," but most of those words were relatively meaningless to me.

All I knew was she'd been gone, and I was glad she was back. I wanted to ask her to keep an eye out for Mr. Cool Cat. Maybe she could ask The Wrangler if he knew what happened to him. And I'd give her this shiny thing, whatever it was. Bipeds liked shiny things even more than cats.

Before long, I heard Cat's voice floating on the air as she emerged from the building with Gloria by her side. "Well, I'm glad Mr. Forest wasn't too upset. He's going to have Security look at it before deciding whether or not to call the police. I wonder if the package was actually delivered by the mail carrier, or if the sender dropped it off on the doorstep? They have a security camera, right?"

Her sidekick started to reply, but I raced out from the bush with the trinket in my mouth and rubbed against her legs. She held on to the railing as she crouched down closer to me.

"Zoe! Hey, stranger! What's that in your mouth?" She reached out her hand, and I dropped the shiny object into her palm.

She rose back up and showed my present to her friend. "Hey, look what Zoe just gave me!"

"Can we talk?" I interrupted before they had time to discuss the present any further. "I'm glad you're back and all, and I just found that and thought it was pretty. But I actually do need your help."

"This isn't a great place to chat, Zoe. Another custodian will probably come out of the building or come around the corner any second. Can we meet later?" She leaned back down again to pet me, her hand gliding along the thick gray fur on my back. I arched into her, a purr rumbling in my throat.

I had momentarily forgotten the pressing issue I needed to discuss with her. "Hey, I'm looking for Mr. Cool Cat," I blurted out as she withdrew her hand and straightened to her full height. "I'll find you later, when it's dark. Just be on the lookout for him, will ya?"

"Sure, of course. That's the older light gray tabby, right?"

"That's Cool," I confirmed. "Catch ya later."

I scampered off into the burgeoning dusk. Hopefully we'd get a chance to have a proper conversation later tonight.

CATHERINE

Seeing Zoe warmed my heart, and I certainly wasn't expecting a gift. I handed it directly over to Gloria while Zoe told me about her missing friend. We'd only been clocked in for a couple hours at this point, so I hadn't seen any of the cats yet. It was a little early in the evening for them to make their appearance.

"This is a pretty necklace," Gloria said, still examining the piece. "She said she found it here in the park? Probably fell off someone on one of the rides."

"Can I see it?" I held out my hand, and she dropped the silver pendant on a matching chain into it. "Oh, it's a locket!" I realized there was a seam between the two sides of the oval, and I popped it open with my thumbnail. "Wait, I need my glasses to see this properly." I fished them out of the fanny pack I wore around my waist while I was at work.

"Well, what's on the inside?" Gloria crowded around me, trying to get a look of her own.

I was expecting to see two lovers, one on each side, or maybe baby pictures, but— "Huh, that's an interesting image to put in a locket. Usually it's a photo, you know?"

"Well, what is it?" Gloria's face scrunched up as she tried to get a closer look.

"It looks kind of like a tiny painting." I held it out from my face, trying to determine the best distance away from my eyes to make out the details. "I still can't see it very well. Don't we have a magnifying glass in the lounge?"

"I think so. A painting? What kind of painting?" Her curiosity was obviously piqued. We'd just gotten back to work, and we already had a mystery to solve. Hey, at least it wasn't a dead body this time.

We climbed the three steps to the door and headed back down the hall of the facility services building to the employee lounge. A couple of our coworkers were taking an early dinner break, their meals spread out across a rickety card table on paper towels that featured a fall leaves motif.

"Look, even the paper towels are festive!" Alan said, his face lighting up with a charming grin. He was the senior member of our shift at the ripe old age of seventy-three. We kept asking him when he was going to retire, and he usually answered that he'd retire when he was dead.

"What'cha got there?" his companion, Pete, asked. He was about a decade younger than Alan. Neither of the two men was as spry and agile as Gloria and I. They tended to take a lot of breaks and occupy the lounge a little longer than they should. Our former boss let it slide. I wasn't sure how long Sheri was going to turn a blind eye.

"Oh, we found a necklace outside," I shared. "It's a locket, actually. Trying to get a look at the painting inside."

"Painting?" Alan's eyebrows arched, and interest was written all over his face. "I'm a bit of an art buff. What kind of painting is it?"

"Well, hold on now, I'm trying to see it. I was gonna use the magnifying glass here in this drawer." I pointed to the drawer, but Gloria had already fished it out and was waving it around victoriously.

She handed it over with a smug smile, and I laid the locket on the counter, directly under a light, and held the magnifying glass at the right distance and angle to see the details of the painting, which was no bigger than an inch long and three-quarters of an inch wide.

"It's an old-fashioned-looking painting of a woman," I announced. My three companions were heavily invested in my assessment of the art.

"What kind of woman?" Alan scratched the silver stubble on his chin.

"Well, it looks like a young white lady. She's tilted back a little, lying on a pillow, and she's wearing a headdress with white roses around it. Her eyes are closed like she's asleep." I moved the magnifying glass away and looked up at my three coworkers. "What an odd thing to put in a locket!"

"Can I see it?" Pete stood up from the card table and sucked in his gut as he edged around Gloria to reach me.

"Sure." I handed him the magnifying glass.

"For some reason, it looks familiar to me, but I can't place it," he said after taking a long, hard look at it.

"Can I see now?" Alan's chin jutted out with determination, as though it were up to him to solve this mystery. "I know a bit about art, you see. Took some classes and did some reading and such."

"Go ahead." Pete handed him the magnifying glass without waiting for any feedback from me.

Alan bent down and hovered the magnifying glass over the locket, his lips twisting as he stared. "I know this painting," he said. "It's *The Dead Bride*."

"Oh! Yes, she's a bride!" I shrieked. "It's a well-known painting?" I clarified. "She's dead?!"

"Well, I don't know about well-known," Alan said, "but around here it's probably more famous than elsewhere since the subject was a real bride who was getting married at St. Michael's Church in Charleston."

Prickles erupted on my forearms as I remembered what Mr. Forest had just said about the assistant GM's daughter working at St. Michael's. Then I remembered the reason I was in Mr. Forest's office in the first place—to show him the bouquet with the creepy note—and dead flowers.

Dead bride. Dead flowers.

Were the bouquet and the locket related? It would be an awfully big coincidence...

Gloria's eyes were like saucers as she elbowed me, her mouth opening and closing like a fish out of water.

"Oh, yeah, her ghost haunts St. Michael's!" Pete chimed in. "I've heard that story."

"Her ghost?" I stammered.

"Yeah..." Alan scratched his chin for a moment as though he were trying to dredge up some distant memory. "I don't remember the whole story...but it's a pretty famous one in Charleston lore. Do you remember the bride's name, Pete?"

"Hmm." He tapped his foot on the tile floor. "Nope. Can't say that I do."

"Well, that's very interesting. I wonder why someone was wearing a locket with that painting in it in the park." I snatched the necklace up and stuffed it in my fanny pack. Did a tourist pick it up as a souvenir while visiting the area?

How creepy is that? Wearing a locket with a picture of a dead bride.

Gloria finally found her voice. "Maybe someone left it outside the facilities services building for a reason. It wasn't found randomly dropped near a ride. It was in an area where guests aren't allowed."

I whipped to face her and immediately shot her a look that conveyed, *DO NOT SAY ANOTHER WORD*. After so many years of working together, we were experts in reading each other's facial expressions.

The two men seemed to be completely clueless about our nonverbal communication. They both cleaned up the remains of their dinner and ambled toward the door, mumbling something about how they ought to get to work.

Once they were gone, and we heard the door to the building close, we both stared at each other for a few moments before Gloria broke the silence. "Do you think the bouquet and the necklace are messages for...us?"

I waved a hand at her, dismissing that theory. "Surely not. No one knew we were at the Forests' beach house except for them and a few of our work friends. It's not like the whole park knew. It makes a lot more sense that the bouquet was for the Forests."

"Maybe," Gloria tapped her fingers on the counter where the magnifying glass still lay, "but don't you think it's a little suspicious that we're getting ready to host a wedding at the park—the wedding of an employee's daughter, who works at St. Michael's Church—and we now have a bridal bouquet of dead flowers and a locket with a painting of a dead bride who supposedly haunts the same church?"

"Well, when you put it like that...it does sound a little suspicious..." I ran my fingers through my hair, trying to avoid the headache that was tap dancing on my temples. "I guess this could be the start of something potentially bad for the park? So you think it has to do with the wedding?"

"Mr. Forest told us to be vigilant, to report any anomalies we find," Gloria reminded me. "I would say this locket goes hand in hand with the bouquet as being weird."

"Like you said, it wasn't found in a guest area but here." My brain was spinning wildly as I tried to figure this out. "Zoe did say she found it right outside our building..."

"Did she say that?" Gloria sighed and adjusted the hem of her tunic. She was wearing leggings with a vibrant palm leaf pattern tonight and a matching green top. A green scarf was wrapped artfully around her head, protecting her springy black-and-gray coils.

"She also said she wants to talk to us later tonight...so let's just wait till the park closes and go find her."

"Good idea," Gloria agreed. "And, meanwhile, we can keep our eyes peeled for any other clues."

I started to push my cart down the hall. "Why do I feel like I'm on an episode of *Scooby Doo*? They said this dead bride was a ghost. A ghost, Gloria. Zoinks!"

Four

So did you see your precious biped?" Moony asked when I returned to our territory near the central courtyard.

"I talked to Cat, if that's what you mean." My tail twitched as I sat staring at him. "Where did everyone go?"

"Mousing. We're hungry." Moony crossed one paw over the other and bent to inspect his claws, which looked impressively sharp. "I'm about to go on a hunt as well."

"No, you're coming with me," I insisted. "We have to find Cool. He's been missing for a while now, and I'm really worried about him."

"You should just let him go, Sis. He's old. He's feeble. He probably went off to die alone so he doesn't burden the clowder."

"He wouldn't leave without saying goodbye," I argued. "C'mon. The park is closed now; we can go wherever we want. I want to check out the woods. I've heard a lot of commotion coming from there all day. What if he's trapped or something and can't get out?"

"How would he get trapped?" Moony tilted his head, peering at me.

"There's a fence around that whole area, duh. What if he went in when the gates were open, and now he can't get out? He could be tired and hungry and weak. We might need to get in there and help him out. He can't climb the fence in his condition."

My brother huffed. "Whatever."

"We don't leave anyone behind," I reminded him. "That's not what family does."

"It's probably his time," he repeated his theory from earlier, "but whatever you say. You're in charge."

That's more like it.

I took off toward the back of the park, and he fell in rhythm next to me, our paws pounding on the sidewalks across grassy knolls as we raced each other. He pulled slightly ahead, and I let him. I had learned it was good to let other people think they won sometimes—it meant less resistance when you needed to win more important battles.

The gates to the woods were wide open when we arrived, and biped workers were everywhere. "Stay low, out of sight, Moony."

Though the Fairytale Forest employees knew about us and our function in the park, they were encouraged to keep their distance. We all knew that too much biped-feline interaction would lead to our being evicted from the park. That had already happened to Moony a few months ago when Scar and his thugs set him up to be captured by the park's cat wrangler. If it wasn't for Cat, Moony wouldn't have made it back. He would have been adopted into some family's home as a house cat.

Eww. Trapped inside with boring kibble and the same

four or five bipeds, day in and day out. Not a mouse in sight. *No thank you!*

That was not the life any of us wanted. We may have had constraints here in Fairytale Forest, like staying out of sight during the times when guests were in the park, but we had all the freedom we wanted when the park was closed.

"What's going on in there?" Moony stopped, out of breath, his tongue hanging out like a dog's as he surveyed what was going on beyond the open gates.

Dozens of bipeds in yellow vests were racing about with ladders—*pretty sure that's what they're called*—and enormous floodlights that made it appear nearly as bright as daytime inside the woods area. They also had motorized equipment that lifted them to tall heights in the trees. It looked like they were wrapping the tree branches with tiny lights.

"I believe they're decorating," I said with confidence. "That's the word for it."

"Decorating?" Moony stared at me. "What the fluff does that mean?"

"Oh, you know bipeds. They're always celebrating something. They have holidays, you know. Don't you remember them putting out different objects at different times of the year? It's getting colder. I think it's the time of year when they use pumpkins and other motifs to celebrate the shorter days and longer nights."

My brother's whiskers twitched as he listened to me. "Motifs? Do you even hear yourself, Sis? You sound like one of them."

"I've spent a lot of time immersed in biped culture," I reminded him. "Remember how the security bipeds used to feed me treats and let me hang out with them? I don't know how I avoided getting deported from the park, to be honest. Must be because I'm so awesome."

"Uh-huh, I'm sure that's it. Probably because they knew

no family was gonna adopt you out of a shelter," he fired back. "They took pity on your furry butt."

I narrowed my eyes at him. "That's just mean."

"Well, they obviously didn't think I was unlovable. Your biped pal rescued me before a family got to come choose me." He puffed out his chest.

"Say the word, and we can arrange for you to go back to the shelter," I advised him.

"Oh, look!" he ignored me. "The lights are pretty!"

In the time we'd been arguing, the bipeds had magically turned on all the trees. Some had green lights, some purple, and some looked a dark amber color, like tiny flames. "I don't remember them ever doing that before."

"Me either."

"I wonder what's different this year?" I stepped a bit closer, trying to get a better look. "Let's try to slip by them when they aren't looking. I still can't help but think Cool might be in here somewhere, and maybe he just can't find a way out on his own."

Moony followed me to a tree right outside the gates that was cast in shadow. I threw him a look over my shoulder, and he understood what I was suggesting. We raced in sync through the gates to a clump of bushes far away from the massive beams of light being projected through the woods.

"Do you smell him?" I sniffed the air, encouraging my brother to do the same.

We both prowled around the area, racing from shadow to shadow to search for our missing clowder member. I didn't like doing it when there were so many bipeds around, but they definitely weren't paying attention to us. We both felt the earth rumble under our paws as another huge machine rolled through the gates with a big bucket on the front and some sort of enormous claw on the back. Then another followed with an attachment on the front. It had the girth of a tree and resembled a drill. It pierced the earth near the gate and began to growl as it twisted itself deep into the ground.

"What the mouse turds are they doing?" Moony practically vibrated with fear as the sound of the machines drowned out our own thoughts and heartbeats.

"I don't know; stay down," I warned. If Mr. Cool Cat was trapped in here, he was likely so scared, he was frozen. But I hadn't been able to pick up his scent anywhere.

"Maybe we should go. I don't like this at all," my brother said when the machine shut off for long enough to move to a different spot before it began to drill again.

"Fine, fine," I capitulated. "We'll come back tomorrow night. Hopefully they'll be done."

Workers were hoisting huge poles, twisting them down into the holes the machine had dug. We slipped by a group of yellow-vested bipeds with their backs to us, but I noticed a tiny white card on the ground, standing out against the freshly dug earth.

There was a cross on the white card and a picture of what looked like a tower with windows on it. There were biped markings on it too—words—I just didn't know how to read them. I'd take it to Cat and see if it was important. I had seen that cross marking before. I just couldn't remember what it meant.

"C'mon!" Moony threw over his shoulder, scowling at me as I stopped to examine the card. I snatched it up between my teeth, and we ran for cover on the other side of the gates.

CAT

I turned the card that Zoe had left me under my custodial cart over in my hand. I saw her drop it there when I was coming out of the restroom after cleaning, and then she scampered off before someone could see her. "There's writing on the back: 1015. What do you think that means?"

Gloria took the card from me and adjusted her reading glasses. "Charlotte Carson—that's Tom's daughter, right? Mr. Forest said she's the communications director at St. Michael's. It's her business card?"

"It appears to be. Maybe she dropped it when she was visiting the park. I just wondered if you had any ideas what the numbers hand-written in blue pen on the back could be. Those are ones, right? Not sevens? They have little flags at the top."

"Could it be the time of a service? 10:15?" Gloria peered closer. "If it's really a thousand and fifteen, you'd think the person could just remember it. Wasn't there some psychological experiment that claimed people can remember up to seven numbers easily, and that's why phone numbers are seven numbers?"

"Hmm. Perhaps. Writing down a time seems likely but there's no colon between the zero and second one. Do you think we should show this to Mr. Forest?"

"I know he said he wants to be notified of anything unusual, but is a business card unusual?" Gloria shrugged. "Mr. Carson works here in the park and could have dropped it out of his briefcase or pocket or something. Or maybe Charlotte was here and dropped it."

"She's the one getting married," I noted. "Add this to the other weird stuff, the bridal bouquet of dead flowers and the locket with a dead bride in it. Maybe these *are* clues for a... murder?" I whispered the last word.

"Catherine!" Gloria hissed my full name. "First off, be careful saying that word around here. And second, don't you think your imagination is running a little wild? The other two murders have been employees. She's not."

"But her dad is. And she's getting married in the park. Mr. Forest specifically said we need to make sure nothing is left to chance. This wedding has to go off without a hitch—or another you-know-what." I avoided the M word just for her.

"Well, what are you suggesting we do?" Gloria's eyes darted around the vicinity, making sure we were alone.

"Well, her office hours are listed. What if we just go pay her a visit? We can say we're working on making her wedding the best event of the year at Fairytale Forest. We can say we're like wedding ambassadors or something."

Gloria scoffed. "Where do you come up with these crazy ideas, woman?" She tsked. "I don't know about you sometimes."

"So, are you in or what?" I looked down at my silver watch. "It's almost time to clock out. We could go home, shower, change, and head into Charleston?"

"Tell ya what," she pursed her lips like she was ready to make a deal, "I'll go with you to St. Michael's if you agree to brunch at Poogan's Porch." It was a cute little restaurant in an old house in the historic district.

"Oh, yum!" I rubbed my belly. "I could definitely go for some chicken and waffles!"

"I thought that might appeal to you." Gloria grinned.

Five

CATHERINE

After Gloria nearly gave me a heart attack by squeezing into the tiniest parallel-parking space in the city in her little silver Mercedes, we stuffed our faces full of chicken and waffles at Poogan's Porch. Then we dragged our full bellies a couple of blocks up Meeting Street to St. Michael's. The downtown church was used to getting tons of visitors, so no one even glanced our way when we went inside.

I hadn't been in the building before, and I was a little taken aback by the vast space. A wide aisle in a checkerboard pattern divided the sanctuary in half, leading to an altar draped with a white cloth and a cross emblem. Huge wood columns and sturdy pews rose up symmetrically. The back wall was dominated by an enormous arched stained-glass window that depicted Saint Michael slaying a dragon, based on a famous painting by Raphael that hangs in the Louvre.

Okay, I didn't know that, but Gloria and I gained this newfound knowledge by blending in with a tour group getting a lecture from a docent at the side of the church. As soon as the tour group moved on, I noticed another staff member stayed behind. She was a petite white woman with neatly coiffed white hair, wearing a large gold cross that contrasted nicely with her light mauve sweater.

I stepped up to greet her, a friendly smile on my face. "Good morning! We're looking for Charlotte Carson. Do you know where her office is?"

"Are you members of the congregation?" She blinked a few times as she lightly fingered the cross pendant that fell at the midpoint of her chest.

"No, ma'am," Gloria took over. "We're from Fairytale Forest and need to discuss her wedding arrangements with her. We've been sent by the Forests."

Oooh, good one, G!

The woman smiled. "Yes, that's right. Miss Carson will be getting married soon. Here, I'll show you to her office." She gestured toward the back of the sanctuary, and we followed her slowly down the checkerboard aisle.

"Down that hall, up the stairs, third door on your right," she directed us with two fingers pointing to her left.

"Thank you so much! Have a wonderful day!" I said before we headed down the hall.

"God bless," she called after us.

We climbed the stairs and headed to the third door on the right side of the hallway. It was open, and when we peered inside, a young woman with reddish-brown hair, wearing a conservative ivory swiss-dot blouse, was seated at a desk, typing away at a keyboard attached to a computer. She noticed us out of her peripheral vision and held up a single finger to ask us to give her a moment. She was obviously concentrating on something.

We waited a few minutes as her fingers click-clacked on the keys much faster than I could ever imagine typing. Then she looked up, smiled, and beckoned us inside. "Hi, should I have been expecting you?" she greeted us with a warm, genteel Southern accent.

"Hi, Charlotte, I'm Catherine Lyon, and this is Gloria Bress. We're from Fairytale Forest. We work with your dad." That might have been a bit of a stretch, but I needed her to trust me, and I knew Mr. Forest would vouch for us if needed. This was the whole "ask for forgiveness rather than permission" thing, right?

"Oh, hi!" Her face lit up, and she pressed her hands together with a wide grin spreading her full pink lips. It was impossible to miss the enormous diamond solitaire ring on her left hand. "What can I do for y'all?"

"We're here to touch base with you about the wedding," I explained and glanced over at Gloria. She nodded and flashed me an encouraging smile. We probably should have planned our strategy out a little better over breakfast, but those waffles—well, they inspired a lot more *yums* than they did a gameplan.

"Oh, great!" Then she frowned. "But...uh...my wedding coordinator isn't here?"

"Wedding coordinator?" I swallowed the lump in my throat. "Oh, we weren't told about a—"

"Yeah, her name is Marci. Marci Beauchamp. Should've been on the paperwork I filed with the events office at Fairytale Forest. Should I call her...or?"

Gloria and I exchanged a confused look, and Gloria took up the mantle. "If she can participate by phone, that'd be—"

"Oh, well, she works at Society Hall just down the street. I could see if she can pop over?" Charlotte suggested but pulled out her phone, and her thumbs went flying before we agreed. She finished and looked up from her phone. "She's still a little miffed that we aren't getting married over there—"

We both looked at her with curious expressions.

"Over at Society Hall, or even here with the reception over there. My parents aren't thrilled about it either. Nor are they happy about the Halloween theme. It was my fiancé's idea. He grew up going to Fairytale Forest, and, well, he's like a big kid at heart. He loves dressing up, and as soon as we got serious, he said he wanted to get married in the park. I don't know what Dad's so grumpy about. It's costing him a lot less to have it there. It's not like he has to pay to rent it out or anything. Society Hall is pricy!"

She giggled and looked down at her phone when it dinged. "Okay, she's on her way over. Can I get you two some coffee or water?"

"Oh, water would be great, thanks," Gloria spoke up.

When Charlotte headed out, my comrade immediately turned her whole body toward me and mouthed, "What the heck are we doin' here, sugarbun?"

"I don't know!" I mouthed back. "But I'll think of something."

"You better not frighten that poor girl," Gloria whispered. "Bless her heart, she seems so young! And naïve."

I nodded. She sure did. What was she, twenty-three? Twenty-four? She was barely out of college, as far as I could tell.

"And don't forget to ask her about the Dead Bride," she reminded me. "Preferably without scaring the stuffing out of her!"

"Right, right." I patted my purse to remind us both that I carried the pendant Zoe found. I'd put it in a tiny black velvet pouch for safekeeping.

Before we had the chance to conspire further, the sound of heels click-clacking on the tile floor echoed down the hall. I didn't remember Charlotte's shoes making that sound when she left, so I was not entirely surprised when a heavily perfumed blur of fuchsia chiffon that contrasted with Charlotte's modest and subdued dress click-clacked into the office.

The twenty-something woman stopped mid-stride and stared at us. She probably didn't expect to see two older ladies sitting in her client's office, one of whom (me) was dressed rather unfashionably (as usual) in denim capri pants and a faded purple polo shirt. "Um, hello?"

"Hi, I'm Cat, and this is Glor—" I started to introduce us as Charlotte rushed in carrying two bottles of water.

"Marci!" she shrieked in her shrill voice. "They're here about the wedding. I didn't want you to miss out." She handed us the water bottles and plopped down in her chair behind the desk.

"Thanks." The blonde, whose shape was somewhat obscured by layer after layer of frothy pink skirts, placed her hands on her hips. At least I assumed her hips were under there somewhere. "Where am I supposed to sit?" she pouted.

"Grab one of the chairs across the hall from the meeting room," Charlotte suggested in her rich-as-honey Southern drawl.

Marci looked none too pleased at the idea of carrying a chair, but she huffed and click-clacked her way through the task. She brought the chair to Charlotte's side of the desk and lowered herself into it stiffly. "Now, what is this meeting all about?" she said, almost accusingly. "I didn't have it on my calendar."

"Well, Mr. Forest just wants to make sure everything goes smoothly on Charlotte and…uh…what's your fiancé's name, dear?" I smiled warmly at the bride.

"It's Walker, ma'am. Walker Buckley," she answered, the smile gracefully curling her lips never wavering.

"We want Charlotte and Walker to have a special day," I

leaned toward Marci, hoping to assure her we were on their side.

"Right, well, with everything that's happened at the park lately, it's understandable," Marci said matter-of-factly.

Now Charlotte's smile finally fell, and her hand jerked to her mouth as she gasped. "Marci, you shouldn't be talking about that!" She glanced at her wedding coordinator with a horrified look and then back to us with an apology in her eyes.

"Oh, we are well aware," I assured them both. "I know it's not public knowledge—"

"You mean about the employees being found dead on property?" Marci looked down at her nail as if her question was the most casual one she'd ever uttered.

"Wait!" Charlotte cut off the answer that was about to stammer out of me. "I know who you are! You're the lady who figured out the murderers. I heard my dad talk about you. Catherine Lyon—that's your name, right?"

I nodded. I never dreamed she'd know who I was. That certainly complicated our mission.

"Yes. So…anyway," I decided to just come clean at this point, "Mr. Forest asked us to be on the lookout for anything that seemed out of place in the park. We just don't want anything to interfere with your special day."

Charlotte brought both of her hands to her heart and gave a dopey sigh. "That's so sweet!"

"We have had a couple of interesting things pop up in the past week, so I wanted to tell you about them and see if you think they might be connected to your wedding. Probably not—it's likely just a coincidence, but…well, Mr. Forest said we can't be too careful."

Charlotte looked a little cautious now, glancing over at Marci then wringing her fingers together.

"Like what?" Marci demanded.

"Well, first off, we were staying at the Forests' beach house on Isle of Palms, and we had a box delivered with no address label or anything, and inside was this…" I took out my phone and flipped through the photos—there weren't many—until I came to the ones of the decaying bouquet.

Both of Charlotte's hands flew to her mouth to stifle her gasp when she saw the note attached to the faded roses. "'You're next'?! What does that mean? Who does that mean?"

Gloria's foot swept over to tap mine, but she kept her dark eyes focused on the two younger ladies. I could pretty much read her mind: *So much for not scaring the stuffing out of the poor thing.*

I swallowed hard and tried to make it sound less terrorizing. "To be honest, we weren't sure if it was meant for the Forests or for us, since we were staying there, but almost no one knew we were there. It appears to be a bridal bouquet, and you're getting married, so—"

"I…I used to stay at the Forests' beach house with Jocelyn when I was growing up. She—she's my matron of honor," Charlotte stammered. Jocelyn was the Forests' middle child and only daughter.

"What else did you find?" Marci snapped. I expected her to comfort her client, who looked visibly shaken by this conversation, but she ignored Charlotte and was glaring at us instead.

"Well," I pulled the velvet bag out of my purse, "we found this in the park. It wasn't dropped like someone just lost it on a ride. It was hanging from the branch of a bush like someone put it there on purpose." I opened the drawstring and dumped the locket out on her desk.

With trembling fingers, Charlotte picked it up and studied it. "A necklace?"

"It's a locket," Gloria explained. "It has a picture inside."

"A painting," I elaborated. "One that has to do with this church, if I understand it correctly."

Charlotte carefully pulled the locket apart, and this time an "Eeep!" pierced the stillness of the room. She stood up and paced behind her desk. "Harriet Mackie," she said, "she was to be married here in 1804. She wasn't feeling well, so she lay down in the room just across the hall from here. She died before she could get married. The church keeps a gold cross in that window in her memory to this very day…"

Gloria and I exchanged looks. "I'm sorry if this is upsetting, Charlotte. We just want to know if you have any idea who might want to interfere with your wedding. It almost seems like they're taunting you—or us. We're not sure why. Maybe it's just all in good fun?"

"I don't understand what this has to do with Charlotte," Marci interjected. "The bouquet was delivered to the Forests' beach house. The necklace was found in the park. If they wanted to target Charlotte, why wouldn't they have done so directly?"

"Good question. We found one more thing. Your business card with the numbers '1015' written on the back in blue pen. Does that number mean anything to you?" I dug in my purse and retrieved the card in question, laying it in front of her on the desk.

She shook her head. "That's my card, but I have no idea what 1015 is…" Then her eyes grew wide. "Unless it's October fifteenth—that's the date of the wedding."

Marci snatched it up and examined it. "It isn't written like a date. It probably doesn't have anything to do with her wedding. Anybody could have dropped it in the park. Heck, her dad might have dropped it."

"Well, we're trying to figure out what to make of these strange clues," I admitted. "We don't know if these things are related, but Mr. Forest doesn't want anything else to go wrong in the park. So that's why we're here. To see if we're missing anything—a piece of the puzzle—that might help us determine if someone is threatening you, the park, the wedding, the Forests…

"You haven't noticed anything strange, have you?" Gloria asked Charlotte. "Gotten any strange packages or notes?"

Charlotte's fingers stroked down her throat as she stopped pacing and faced her desk, her head shaking back and forth. "I…I just don't know why anyone would want to mess with me," she sobbed. "I try so hard to make everyone happy! Why would—"

Now Marci leapt up from her seat and drew the younger woman into her arms, patting her back stiffly. She looked over Charlotte's shoulder at us. "Y'all need to move along. You had no right comin' in here and disturbin' my client's peace. Look how upset you've made her!"

"We're only trying to help," I insisted, but Gloria flashed me a look that said we needed to get going.

"Go on, get!" She shooed us away like we were dogs trying to steal food off a table.

"Charlotte, if you think of anything that might be helpful, or if anything odd or suspicious happens, please let us know, okay? You can call Mr. Forests' office, and he will get you in touch with us." I stood up, and Gloria patted my arm. "We'll get out of your hair for now. Take care of yourself, okay, darlin'?"

"Thanks for your time," Gloria added. "I'm sure everything will go just swimmingly on your big day!"

Six

"Ready to go search the woods again?" I nudged Moony when he returned from hunting with Ziti, Amber and Ice.

"Not really." He stretched out on the grass, crossing one paw over the other.

"I'll go with you," Amber offered. "I haven't been in the woods for a long time, and I know the bipeds are doing a lot in there. I chased a mouse almost to the gates last night."

"Yeah, take Amber," Moony agreed. "I'm tired. I wanna rest."

I huffed, "Fine, whatever. We'll be back." I turned my gaze on Amber. "Let's go."

One disadvantage of taking Amber was that her light-yellow fur wouldn't be as easy to hide as my gray fur and Moony's mostly gray fur. "You're gonna have to be stealthy, got it?"

She licked her lips. "I can be stealthy."

We raced toward the back of the park then took cover in

the same bushes Moony and I had hidden in the night before. "You haven't heard anything about Cool, have you?" I asked my soldier. "Maybe from a tom or molly from a different clowder?"

She straightened her spine and tilted her head just slightly like it would help her remember. "Not about Cool, no."

"Well, did you hear some dirt about something else? C'mon, Amber, you know you're supposed to bring me any intel. Do you want to make our clowder less safe? The park less safe? There's been a lot of turmoil and upheaval due to these recent biped deaths. Now is not the time to get complacent."

My words were obviously too big for her. She wasn't the sharpest claw on the paw, after all. Sharper than Daisy, but that wasn't saying much. She just stared at me, blinking, until I shook my head. "Did you see something?"

"Well, maybe…" She blinked sheepishly like she had to contemplate whether or not to tell me.

"Spill it," I commanded.

"Okay, it's probably nothing, but…"

"But what?" She was really starting to aggravate me. This was the last time I let her tag along on an important mission. I needed soldiers I could trust. Not whatever this wishy-washy bit she was giving me right now was.

"I saw Snow talking to Vinny," she blurted out.

"Are you kidding me?" I tapped a paw on the ground, my claws springing out as rage flared in every cell of my body. "Where? What were they talking about?"

Since Snow helped us humiliate Scar, Vinny, and the rest of the Mafia Cats after the last murder in the park, he'd been scarce. I was giving Snow some space because it was his biped who'd been murdered. He'd been around just enough that I hadn't worried about him, and he seemed to dote on me whenever we crossed paths. But he should know better than to associate with Vinny, Scar's right-hand tom.

"Um…they were by the tree. This was last night when you and Moony were here. I didn't hear their conversation," she admitted. "Sorry. Could have been nothing." She raised both paws innocently, her wide amber eyes—the source of her name—beseeching me not to be angry with her.

"Thanks for telling me," I finally said. We'd have to work on her spying skills. "In the future, let me know immediately if you see Snow cavorting with any other sworn enemies, will ya?"

"Sure thing, Boss." Her lips spread into what was sort of a smile, at least by cats' standards. "Oh, wow, I just noticed all the lights in the trees. They're so pretty!"

"I'll have to ask Cat what they're planning in here. I don't remember them decorating this extensively in the other seasons I've been here." I looked around—they'd added quite a few things since we'd been here last.

Amber shook her head. "Me either. Ooh, what are those over there?"

The ground was a bit foggy—probably mist coming off the river. Some three-dimensional but flat-ish stones rose up from a clearing between the trees. They had biped markings on them, but obviously I couldn't read them. "These look kind of creepy, don't they?"

Amber gave a single nod.

Why did bipeds enjoy being scared? From my time hanging out with the security bipeds, I knew how much they loved suspenseful, thrilling entertainment. Some even liked to witness death, blood, homicidal maniacs and other frightening things—but only if they were pretend.

Cats don't enjoy being scared. But bipeds loved scaring us and watching us practically jump out of our fur. From what I could tell, they only liked fake fright or frightening others. I was pretty sure the decorations in the woods met both criteria.

Bipeds are so weird.

"Look for any signs of Cool." I sniffed the air. "I don't smell him, but that doesn't mean he's not here. There's a thick odor of biped here."

The bipeds we saw the night before were no longer around, but they had built a new area with these marked-up stones and, beyond that, what looked like a massive stone table with an arch behind it. The arch was woven from huge ornate vines, popping with blooms the color of blood and twinkling with the same green, purple, and orange lights artfully arranged in the trees. I didn't remember any of this stuff being here before or in previous years.

We crept around the stones with markings on them until I stopped dead in my tracks. There was a small object perched on top of one of the stones. It was black and had what looked like a little hat with a crown on top of it. I remembered the silver figurine I found that turned out to be a major clue in the murder case Cat was trying to solve. Could this small figure also be important?

"Hey, what do you think that is?" I asked Amber, despite knowing there was about a zero percent chance she'd be able to ID it.

"No clue. Some biped thing. You know how they love little pieces of junk." She swiped a paw toward the object. "Why, you think it belongs to your biped friend?"

"Who, Cat? No…doesn't belong to her, but she might find it interesting. I'm going to take it to her. I gave her something shiny yesterday, and she seemed quite enthralled by it." I had the feeling Cat was a loyal biped, but it didn't hurt to try to keep her on my good side.

Never know when I might need her help again.

"I don't see any signs of Cool anywhere, and I definitely

don't smell him," Amber said as I grabbed the small black object that was about the size of a mouse, maybe a bit smaller, in my mouth.

"You're really gonna carry that around all night?" Amber stared at me, blinking glowing eyes that matched her name.

"No, just until I find Cat."

CATHERINE

"Do you think we're jumping to conclusions and overreacting about the bouquet and locket?" I asked Gloria as we wheeled our carts toward the tree. We had a special assignment tonight to look through the Haunted Wood, which was where the wedding was to take place, and make sure nothing seemed amiss.

Sheri sort of rolled her eyes when she told us Mr. Forest made a call and asked her to give us that task. "I'd planned to have you scrub down the games in the arcade, but what Mr. Forest wants, Mr. Forest gets."

"I think we're being appropriately concerned," Gloria said in that measured way of hers. "We didn't jump to any conclusions. We're just trying to make sense of the evidence."

"Exactly!" I agreed. "I don't know why that Marci woman was so insistent we leave Charlotte's office. We didn't do anything wrong. We have her client's best interests at heart."

"We do," Gloria confirmed. "But does she? That's what I wanna know."

"Right? She very much rubbed me the wrong way. As my son would say, she didn't pass the vibe check." I was pretty sure I used that lingo correctly. "And what in the world was she wearing?"

"She looked like two scoops of raspberry sherbert in that dress!" Gloria shook her head. "I don't know who told her she could, you know?"

I laughed. "I wonder why Charlotte thinks she needs a wedding coordinator. We have an events director here at the park, and I'm sure she does most of the planning for weddings. Not that we usually have weddings here—"

"I think the last one I remember was Jocelyn Forest's!" Gloria tapped her chin as if trying to recall any others.

"The Forests' daughter, right?" Seemed like I'd just heard that name earlier today. "Didn't Charlotte say she was her best friend and matron of honor?"

Gloria nodded. "She sure did. It's interesting both girls wanted to get married here. Also that Charlotte spent a lot of time at the Forests' beach house, which is where we received the bouquet."

"But Jocelyn didn't get married in the Haunted Wood at Halloween, right?" I asked.

"No, ma'am. She got married over by the river. On that bridge...you know, the one they found the last body under."

We both simultaneously shuddered at the memory.

"Well, Charlotte said it was her fiancé's idea to get married in the Haunted Wood, that he loves Halloween and is a big kid at heart," I remembered from our conversation this morning. "He better not be playing a trick on her with all this creepy stuff. No man would do that to the woman he loves, right?"

"Lord Almighty, I hope not! It is interesting, though, that she agreed to his request, especially since she works at one of the most well-known churches in Charleston. She must *really* not want to get married in a church."

The area behind the Tree of Wishes was one of my favorites in the park. It was open and nicely landscaped with evergreen trees. "Well, let's go check out the Haunted Wood and see how they've decorated it for the wedding. I think it's an interesting choice for a wedding venue."

We pushed our carts up to the gate, and I whipped out my ID badge. Mr. Forest had granted us carte blanche access to the park, and, sure enough, whcn I scanned it, there was a low groan and the lock on the gate popped open.

"Wow, look at that technology!" Gloria exclaimed. "The Forests are moving into the new millennium—finally!"

I laughed at her animated expression. "I know! Next thing, they'll have robots to clean the park instead of us!"

"Girl, you better not be putting any ideas in their heads. I'd like to keep this job until I retire. After that, they can bring in all the robots they want." She waved her hands in a big arc to indicate the extent of robots she'd welcome after retirement.

"No, they have to wait until after *I* retire," I corrected her. Then I stopped dead in my tracks. "Wow, look at this place! It looks so cool!" I stepped toward what looked like a stone altar with a large arch of twisted vines, flowers and lights behind it. "Is this where the wedding will be? They made it look like a graveyard!"

"It's creepy as all get out in here." Gloria shivered, wrapping her arms around herself. "What are these gravestones made out of?"

"They look so real, but I'm sure they're not. They can't be. Probably some sort of resin. I wish I had a light so I could read the inscriptions." I started to fish my phone out of my fanny pack so I could use the flashlight, but Gloria looked disturbed.

"Uh, no thank you. Okay, I'm ready to leave now." Gloria's voice trembled as she started heading for the gate.

"Wait!" I called after her. "This stuff really scares you, doesn't it?"

"Well, of course it does, Cat. It's not natural, this occult stuff. Look at that altar. It looks like something out of a durn horror movie! I'm surprised it's not splattered with blood." She shuddered.

"Ahhhhhh!!!!" I screamed when I felt something brush against my legs. I leaped about ten feet into the air, then looked down to see Zoe staring up at me with her wide, glowing green eyes.

Gloria looked like she'd just had a heart attack, bent over, clutching her chest. I rushed over and put a hand on her back. "Are you okay? It's just Zoe. And look, she has a little friend with her. That's…uh…Amber, I think."

"Hey, Cat, Gloria," Zoe greeted me and my coworker, even though she couldn't hear her.

"Sorry, Zoe, I think you gave us both quite a scare. C'mon over here, there's a bench. Gloria, come sit down a spell. Get your heart rate down." I gently tugged Gloria by the elbow until she started to move, then I guided her over to the bench. She sat down with shaky knees and a huff.

Zoe dropped something on the bench next to me. "Found this," she said before sauntering back a few feet and then sitting up tall.

I picked up what looked like a chess piece. "I know nothing about chess. Gloria—do you?"

"Yeah, that's the black king," she said. "I used to play with my husband when he was still with us."

It felt cold in my hand. "Is this marble? It's kind of heavy."

"Tell me about it," Zoe said. "I found it sitting on top of one of those stones over here." She turned her head toward the graveyard.

I flipped the piece over and noticed something on the bottom, but I couldn't tell what it was. "Do you have your phone, Gloria? Left mine in my locker."

She shook her head. "I don't usually carry mine with me.

I'm too afraid of getting it wet or breaking it. Those little buggers are expensive!"

"Yeah, seriously." I slipped the chess piece into my fanny pack. "Not sure if this means anything, but we'll take a look, Zoe. You guys doing okay? Did you find your friend?"

"No, we were here looking for him. I'm pretty worried about him, and cats don't get worried too often." Her tail swished back and forth as she spoke, like she was starting to get agitated.

"I don't blame you. You thought he might have come inside the Haunted Wood?" I cocked my head and stared at her as her tail now wrapped around her body. Her little friend, a light creamy-orange tabby, sat nearby licking her front paw.

"I have no idea. He's getting older, and his mind isn't what it used to be, sadly." Her tail began swishing back and forth again like a metronome. I thought cats did that when they were angry, but maybe they did it out of sadness too.

"That happens to people as well," I assured her. "We're keeping an eye out for him."

"So…" She came a little closer now, right up to my feet. "What is this place? Why did the bipeds make so many changes?"

"Well, for one thing, we're about to celebrate Halloween," I explained.

"What's that?" Zoe asked. "Wait—I feel like I should know this one—"

"It's a fall holiday that celebrates all things to do with death because of everything dying off in preparation for winter. So, there are carved pumpkins and witches and ghosts and zombies and skeletons—all macabre things."

"All what now?" Zoe paced in a circle and sat back down. "You bipeds will celebrate anything, I swear. Who celebrates death?"

"I think it's a way of taking power back from death," Gloria added, though she could only hear my side of the conversation. "It can be a powerful thing. I still find it creepy as all get out, but my ancestors, the Gullah, believed that death is just a new beginning. Different cultures have different ways of dealing with death and grief."

Zoe stared at us, unblinking. "Alright, whatever. I guess I'm never really gonna get it. Cats have nine lives, and we celebrate each one—not death."

"Black cats are celebrated on Halloween," I told her. "Don't you have a black cat in your clowder?"

"Yeah…that would be Sass," Zoe replied, her whiskers twitching. "I don't think I should tell her that she's part of Halloween. She'll be more full of herself than usual."

I couldn't help but laugh at that one. "Oh, the other thing is they're preparing for a wedding here next week."

"A what?"

"A wedding. It's another celebration—not a holiday, but a life event. When two people decide they want to spend their lives together, loving and taking care of each other," I explained.

Zoe spat on the ground. "Yuck, why would anyone want to do that? That sounds terrible. Just two bipeds? Stuck alone together? Forever?"

I chuckled at her reaction. "Well, sometimes they also have kids. You know, make a family together."

She groaned. "I like our way better. Clowders all the way."

Seven

I got back to our headquarters tired and hungry. There was still plenty of night left thanks to the days getting shorter, but I needed a nap more than food. Gallivanting around the park and interacting with Cat and her friend wore me out, even though I liked Cat. It was hard to admit, but my fondness for her was growing.

When I returned, Moony was lazing about with Ziti and Amber while Daisy and Hank argued over which was better to find in the park: ice cream or hot dogs. Kids often dropped whole ice cream cones in the park, leaving a nice thick puddle of sweet goo we enjoyed licking up when we happened to stumble upon it. I felt that hot dogs were more of an acquired taste, but Daisy seemed to prefer them to ice cream. Well, she was wrong. And a ditz, for that matter; but Hank seemed to be reveling in their spirited debate, and it was kind of nice to see him riled up for a change.

"Hey, at least you haven't had to tell Cat about a dead body lately," my brother remarked as I collapsed beside him.

"Yeah, but I have found a couple things she thought might be...signs." I closed my eyes and curled my tail around my body.

"Signs of what?" a familiar voice asked as it approached.

My eyes popped open. "Hey, Snow. Where ya been?"

I hadn't forgotten what Amber told me. Speaking of Amber, she went over to annoy Ziti, batting at her head until her ear twitched, and then she awoke, looking majorly perturbed. Now they were both sitting there watching me interact with Moony and Snow.

"Around," he answered vaguely. Then he picked up something at his side and brought it over to me, dropping it right in front of my nose.

The tantalizing smell lured me to a seated position. It was a nice, fat, juicy mouse. "What's this for?"

"I know you've been looking for Mr. Cool Cat and haven't had a chance to eat. So dig in. My treat." He looked especially proud of himself tonight.

"Wow, thanks, Snow. I appreciate it." I stabbed at the mouse with my claws. It was a fresh kill. Yum.

"So, before you enjoy my gift," he said, his voice smooth and rich, "tell me what you mean by signs. You're talking about your biped friends and their penchant for murder, right?"

I scoffed—or the feline version of it anyway. "My biped friends do not have a penchant for murder, Snow. They have a penchant for *solving* murders. And I don't know if solving two murders really means it's a penchant anyway. I think it's more that they have a penchant for keeping the park open, a goal we should *all* be invested in."

I looked around at the members of my clowder who were present. We were missing Sass, Priss and Cool. Sass and Priss were probably up to no good, and we still didn't know about Cool.

"So, there are signs of another murder?" Snow's ear twitched as he stared me down.

I licked my lips, catching the drool that was appearing thanks to his tasty offering. "There's going to be a wedding in the park, and they want to make sure nothing interferes with it."

"What's a wedding?" Ziti piped up.

"It's when two bipeds want to spend their lives together, and only with each other," I drew from Cat's explanation. "They have a ceremony and a big celebration when they pledge their undying devotion to each other."

"Yuck!" Moony spat, looking entirely disgusted by the concept. Amber joined him with the most nauseated grimace.

"I don't know," Snow threw out, "I think it sounds kind of nice." He took two steps toward me and rubbed his body against mine as he walked in a circle around me.

"It sounds nice to be stuck with just one other biped for your entire life?" Moony asked, sounding like he'd just tasted rancid, rotting flesh. "You know these bipeds live for like seventy or eighty years, don't you? Can you even imagine being stuck with the same stinky biped for that long?"

"My bipeds don't stink," I defended Cat and Gloria. *Oops, where did that come from?*

"So why don't you wedding them?" Moony fired back at me.

"I think the actual term is 'marry,'" I corrected my brother. Speaking of penchants, I had one for correcting him. "But bipeds and felines can't marry. They can only be friends. And I'm fine with that."

"All bipeds stink," Moony snarled. "They are quite gross. Consider the ones who come into the park every day and make a mess out of it. And then your biped and her coworkers, plus all of us, have to clean up after them."

"Well, he does have a point there," Snow agreed, and Moony looked vindicated.

"What do they think is going to happen at this wedding?" Ziti wondered. "Is that what they're planning in the woods where they put up all the lights?"

"Yes," I confirmed, then I addressed her first question. "I think they're worried about another murder. Or anything that might disrupt the wedding. So we have to be extra vigilant. I'm telling Cat every single thing I notice that looks unusual. We've all been here long enough—we know the typical things we find in the park: dropped food, trash, kids' toys and trinkets, and the occasional lost shiny adornment humans wear around their necks, fingers or in their ears. I did find one of those neck-things the other day, and Cat was quite interested in it."

"So we have to look for Cool and anything that might be a sign of an impending murder?" Ziti clarified. "That sounds like too much work. I'm going back to sleep."

"As usual, Ziti is full of wonderful ideas," Amber agreed, and the two settled down near Hank and Daisy, who had finally stopped arguing. Hank was already snoring.

"Fine, whatever. I'm going to go eat this mouse." My clowder was so lazy sometimes. "Thank you, Snow. Did you get enough to eat tonight?"

"Yes, but I'll keep you company." He followed me over to a little nook between two bushes where I liked to hang out.

I took a tentative bite of the mouse, savoring the taste of fresh meat. "This is delicious; thank you for thinking of me."

"It's the least I can do when you work so hard to keep our clowder safe and happy." His gaze roamed down my body.

"Why thank you for noticing, Snow." I preened. "I feel like everyone takes me for granted."

"Not me, Zoe. I would never do that," he purred. "I consider myself very lucky to be here."

"Okay, you better go find something else to do now," I dismissed him. "My whiskers are gonna get too small for my head."

He waved a paw in the air. "It's the truth. You are a very fine leader, Zoe. Very fine indeed." He circled me again, lightly brushing against my fur once more. "In every aspect…"

CATHERINE

"I need to speak with both of you for a minute," Sheri said when we returned to the facility services building at the end of our shift. Her voice followed us down the hall as we went to return our carts to the corral where they'd be restocked before day shift came in.

Gloria nudged me with her elbow and gave me the *now what did we do wrong?* look. I just hoped no one saw us talking to Zoe. I needed to be more careful. I'd already had a slip-up with Jayden, the Forests' son, but thankfully he'd gone off to college a couple months ago.

"What's up?" I poked my head into Sheri's office. She sat at her desk with a huge spreadsheet pulled up on the larger of her two monitors. I couldn't make out what it was for though.

Hopefully not a spreadsheet of our infractions, I thought with a laugh.

"No need to sit. I'll make this quick." She gestured at the door, and Gloria nodded and closed it behind us.

We stood at her desk like obedient puppies, awaiting her next command. I missed Walter, our old boss. He didn't deserve what happened to him, and he was a lot more easy-going than Sheri.

"I just got a call from Mr. Forest's office. He wants you to meet with him and Tom Carson before leaving. Don't bother clocking out. We'll adjust your time cards when you come in tonight. Just head straight over."

"They're waiting for us? In the Guest Services Building?" I checked.

She nodded. "Yes, no more questions. Just go."

I shrugged and looked at Gloria. She nodded, so we said our goodbyes to Sheri and headed toward the front of the park. The morning was brisk, and the sun was just breaking over the horizon. Summer was truly a thing of the past now. There was no turning back. It was going to be shorter days and longer nights until the solstice.

"Do you think we're in trouble?" Gloria asked as soon as we gained some distance. She waved to a few employees heading toward the Tree of Wishes from Storybook Street.

"We better not be," I scoffed. "I don't know how we could be any more proactive."

She grabbed my hand, panic in her voice as she asked, "Do you think Tom knows we went to see his daughter at St. Michael's?"

"Probably. And he probably wants to know why," I theorized. "Maybe Mr. Forest does too. I really think someone is targeting Charlotte, don't you?"

Gloria gave a sad smile along with a nod. "It appears so. Do we think it's Marci? That girl gave me the heebie-jeebies. I don't know why—something about her."

"We need to know more about her," I agreed. "We need to know more about everything having to do with the wedding. Someone is clearly trying to send a message, but why? Is it to target Charlotte or just the Forests in general, since this is their park?"

"Wait..." Gloria's eyes widened. "You don't think the

other murders and…this…this threat to the wedding…are all connected, do you?"

I hadn't considered that before, but…

"Well, let's see," I mulled it over for a moment, "the park has been in operation for, what, forty years, and there was never a death in the park, and then all the sudden, there's been two in the past few months, and both were park employees. That does seem a little unlikely. But they seemed to be completely unrelated. And for the second one, anyway, his death didn't have anything to do with his job."

Gloria shivered as a strong breeze blew down the main street. "I know… It just seems strange to me that, all the sudden, these terrible things are happening here when they never did before."

"But why would someone go after two completely unrelated lower-level employees if who they are trying to hurt is James Forest?" I played Devil's Advocate.

"You're right. It has to be a coincidence. But it does feel like someone is trying to mess with either Charlotte or the Forests with this weird stuff," Gloria pointed out.

"Let's see what Mr. Forest and Mr. Carson have to say. If they think there's something here, maybe they'll give us more access to the wedding plans and party. I'm definitely going to ask about Marci, too."

We had to wait in the small anteroom before Mr. Forest's secretary led us into his opulent office. "Good morning, Catherine, Gloria," he greeted us from behind his beautifully crafted wood desk. I once again admired the lovely photos of his family gracing the bookcases on either side of his desk.

I peered closer at the one of his daughter Jocelyn's wedding. Yes, there was Charlotte, the maid of honor. And who was the best man? He looked familiar.

"Have a seat, ladies. Do you know Tom? Tom, this is

Catherine and Gloria," Mr. Forest introduced the park's assistant general manager.

"Hi, Tom, nice to meet you." Gloria elbowed me when I stood frozen in front of the photo.

"Sorry, I'm stuck on this photo. Mr. Carson, that's your daughter, Charlotte, right? Jocelyn's maid of honor?" I pointed at the picture in a brushed brass frame.

"Yes, ma'am. And Jocelyn will be Charlotte's matron of honor next week at the wedding." Tom Carson had large, waxy jowls, one of those men with a big head and face but a narrow body that didn't match. He extended his hand to me, and I stepped forward to shake it. "They've been best friends since they were knee high to a grasshopper!"

"Let's all go sit over here." Mr. Forest gestured to the sitting area with its leather couches and chairs, arranged cozily around a fireplace that was almost never needed in coastal South Carolina, but it sure did look nice with its marble mantel boasting even more family photos.

"Who is the best man in the photo?" I asked both men. "He looks familiar to me, but I can't figure out why."

"Oh, that's Kenny Davenport," Mr. Forest answered. "He works here—he's the head of landscaping, so you've probably seen him around. He's been good friends with Walker, Charlotte's fiancé, and also Jocelyn's husband, Mark, as well as my son Jamie for years. They all worked here in the park when they were younger, but now Walker works for his dad. Kenny's been promoted a few times since they were all summer workers here."

Both men chuckled and exchanged knowing grins. Jamison Forest, Jayden's older brother, was being groomed to take over the park. Kenny also held a high position. Nepotism at its finest, right?

"I see." I settled into my seat next to Gloria on one of the leather couches and cleared my throat. "You may have heard that we paid Charlotte a visit yesterday morning at St. Michael's."

"Yes, yes. She called me—quite upset—after you left," Mr. Carson admitted. "I don't know why she was so upset, but you know how women are, and being a bride seems to make it about a thousand times worse—"

"Jocelyn was crazy as a betsy bug the whole time she was engaged," Mr. Forest cut him off with a bellowed chuckle. "Janelle and I were about to lose our minds. Fortunately, the wedding went off without a hitch, and she and Mark are so happy together. Now we're waiting for our first grandbaby! They got married at St. Michael's, you know."

"I am surprised Charlotte isn't getting married there as well, since she works there," I observed. "But she said her fiancé has always dreamed of getting married here at Fairytale Forest."

"Indeed," said Mr. Carson. "My wife and I weren't thrilled with the idea, but it is saving us some money, especially since my good friend Jim here is footing the bill!" He and Mr. Forest laughed heartily again. It was the first time I'd ever heard anyone call Mr. Forest "Jim" instead of "James." Even his wife called him James. "So, tell me why you went to visit Charlotte. She was blubbering too much to give me a proper explanation."

"Right. Well, Mr. Forest tasked Gloria and me with keeping an eye out for any…anomalies in the park. Anything that might jeopardize your daughter's wedding day. And, well, first we received what looked like a bridal bouquet of dead flowers with a blood-stained bow. And I understand Charlotte and Jocelyn spent many summers at the Forests' beach house, which is where the bouquet turned up. Then we found a locket in the park with a painting entitled *The Dead Bride,* which depicts a young bride who died just before her wedding at St. Michael's—"

"Oh, yes, Harriet Mackie," Mr. Carson interrupted. "It's a well-known ghost story in Charleston."

"Ahhh…ghosts!" Gloria shuddered beside me.

"Yes," Mr. Forest agreed. "I've heard that one before too."

"Charlotte told us Harriet died before the wedding in one of the rooms on the upper floor of the church. She said there's a gold cross kept in the window of that room in memory of Harriet," I shared.

"I don't remember the whole story, but the carriage companies are quite fond of telling that one on their haunted tours," Mr. Carson revealed.

"Haunted tours?" Gloria looked even more upset by this new information.

"Yes, they give ghost tours in the historic district. Both walking tours and carriage tours. They might even do a haunted boat tour." Mr. Carson's worried gaze bounced from my face to Gloria's and back again. "Do you think the locket being left in the park and the bridal bouquet being sent to Jim and Janelle's beach house has something to do with that story? Like maybe someone is using it to threaten Charlotte? She's the bride, after all." He wrung his hands.

"I'm not sure, to be honest," I answered. "But we're trying to be extra-vigilant, which is why we wanted to talk to Charlotte, to try to find out more about the wedding, who's involved in it, and who might want to try to ruin her big day. How much do you know about this wedding consultant, Marci, we met yesterday? She was pretty upset that we'd come to talk to Charlotte and made us leave before we got the answers we were looking for."

"Well, not much," Mr. Carson replied. "They met in college at C of C. They were roommates their first two years of school, but then Charlotte pledged a sorority that Marci didn't get into."

I glanced at Gloria, who knew exactly what I was thinking.

"Is Marci married?" Gloria asked, completely catching my brainwave.

"She was engaged, but her fiancé called off the wedding this summer," Mr. Carson revealed.

"Anyone we would know?" I piped up.

"Actually, yes, it was Kenny's older brother, Dan." Mr. Carson stroked his clean-shaven chin. "He used to work here as well."

So all of these people knew each other. Interesting—but it certainly made our work that much harder.

"Did Marci ever work in the park?" I asked.

"I can't remember." Mr. Carson shrugged and pulled out his phone. "I'd have to ask Charlotte."

"Hmm, what's her last name?" Mr. Forest's asked. "I'll ask Becky to look her up in the database."

"Good thinkin'," Gloria agreed. "Her last name is Beauchamp, if I remember correctly."

How did she always remember these things? She had more than a decade on me, but her memory was so much sharper than mine.

Mr. Forest went to his desk to make the call, and we all sat quietly. "She'll call me back in a few." He hung the phone up and rejoined us.

"Okay, not only did we find Charlotte's business card just randomly the night before we went to talk to her, but we also found something else tonight when we were looking at the wedding setup in the Haunted Wood." I pulled the chess piece out of my pocket. "It's a king, you know, the piece from a chess set."

I handed it to Mr. Carson first, who barely glanced at it before handing it to Mr. Forest. "I don't know what that would have to do with Charlotte," Mr. Carson said.

"I don't either. But it was sitting on top of one of the tombstones there in the graveyard near the wedding altar. It looked as though it was deliberately placed." Well, that was basically what Zoe told me, anyway.

Mr. Forest's face suddenly went pale. "Did you look at the bottom?"

"No, sorry, sir," I answered as respectfully as I could. "I meant to, but it was dark, and I couldn't see it well at the time."

He thrust it toward us with the bottom of the figure facing out. "It has a tiny owl and the number twenty-two on it." His permanently suntanned skin blanched even whiter. "I live at 22 King Street," he explained. "And we have a stone owl in our doorway."

As soon as he said it, I remembered seeing the owl the one time I visited his house.

And suddenly our suspicions that the bouquet, the locket, the business card, and the chess piece were meant to send a message seemed to be confirmed. What message, though? That was the question.

Eight

CATHERINE

I drove Gloria and myself downtown and parked at a garage near the carriage company where I'd booked a ghost tour. Gloria was not thrilled with the idea, but I promised to take her to dinner at 82 Queen when we were done, which was one of our favorite restaurants in the city.

"I better be in one piece, eating she-crab soup and sipping a martini by eight o'clock," she warned as she climbed out of my Nissan Rogue.

I laughed as I pressed the key fob to lock the doors, then I guided her around the corner to the barn where we met our beautiful Belgian draft horse, Magic. We were ushered right onto the carriage along with a party of six tourists from the North. Judging by their accents, I'd say they were from New York or New Jersey.

Our guide, Dale, promised October was the best time of the year for seeing ghosts in the city. "It's okay if you get scared. Magic and I will protect you!"

Gloria just tightened her vise-like grip on my arm and

gritted her teeth. She was absolutely fearless in so many different respects, I would have never expected the prospect of seeing a ghost would reduce her to a trembling fruit-filled ring of Jello. Hopefully Dale and Magic's offer of protection would alleviate some of her nerves.

The steady clip-clop of Magic's hooves against the Charleston streets was soothing, and the rhythm helped us both settle in for the trip. Dale's voice was deep and booming, full of expression and storytelling flair. Then the moment I'd been waiting for came as we made our way up Meeting Street toward Broad.

Dale had just finished telling us about when the plague struck and Charlestonians were buried in mass graves at the Circular Congregational Church's graveyard. "There's a woman in her late twenties wearing a blue dress that is often seen digging in what was a trench grave used to bury victims of a yellow fever outbreak in 1854. It's said she's looking for her two sons so she can reunite her family."

Gloria shivered beside me as Dale began to describe the beautiful white church all lit up ahead of us: St. Michael's. Yes, we'd just been there during the daytime to speak with Charlotte, but it looked much different now at nighttime.

Dale turned the carriage onto Broad Street and stopped Magic at the side of the church as he began the story of Harriet Mackie. "Harriet was only seventeen years old when she was engaged to marry William Rose. Her wedding day in 1804 was a joyous occasion, contrasting with the painful loss she felt at age twelve when her parents both passed away. Her father owned a vast rice plantation, and his will bequeathed every single penny to his only child, Harriet. She would inherit all of it, either at the age of twenty-two or when she married.

"Unfortunately, shortly before the wedding, after she was dressed and almost ready to walk down the aisle to her groom, she fell ill. She was taken to rest in one of the rooms upstairs in St. Michael's. When someone came back to check on her, she was dead. Poisoned.

"Instead of celebrating a wedding, her groom was left mourning at a funeral for his dead bride. They still keep a cross in the window of the room where she is said to have passed. Many believe her cousin had her poisoned—because he was next in line to inherit her father's plantation.

"So, if you happen to find yourself in St. Michael's grave-yard after dark, be on the lookout for a ghostly apparition in a wedding gown. It is Harriet Mackie, still searching for her groom—and possibly for her killer as well."

Gloria mumbled something as she clutched my arm, and when I turned to look at her as the carriage started up its slow clip-clop again, I saw her eyes were closed. I dared to peer into the graveyard as we passed, but I didn't see any ghosts.

An hour later, we were enjoying our meal at 82 Queen, and Gloria seemed to have recovered from her harrowing experience on the carriage ride. She sipped her cocktail, savoring every drop of it and every spoonful of her she-crab soup.

After that cocktail had a chance to get into my colleague's bloodstream, I thought it safe to return to the mission that brought us to the historic district on a weekday night. "So… what do you think? Is someone using the tale of Harriet Mackie to threaten and taunt Charlotte ahead of her wedding day?"

"To be honest, I wouldn't be surprised if it's that Marci woman," Gloria said. "She seemed miserable. And they almost seem more like rivals than friends. She had a broken engagement, and now her friend is getting married—and she isn't even in the wedding party? But their other friend, Jocelyn, is the matron of honor? It has sour grapes written all over it. Plus, she had a broken engagement…"

"You may be right about that. Maybe we should try to talk to her? Ask her a couple of pointed questions." I tipped back my glass to drain the remainder of my berry mojito.

"Do you think she has access to the park?" Gloria pondered. "The chess piece, the pendant, and the business card were both found inside. They had to have been planted there by someone."

"True…" I rubbed my chin. "I guess we can ask her. Maybe we should get going so we can get some rest tonight, then we can look her up at Society Hall tomorrow. I wonder if we can get a list of the whole bridal party from Mr. Carson? We need to interview all of them. Seems almost everyone has a connection to the park."

"I keep thinking about that bouquet." Gloria dabbed at her mouth with her napkin. "First off—was that really blood on the ribbon? And secondly—what did they mean by 'You're Next'?"

"I keep wondering the same. First I thought it was meant for the Forests. Then when we found the pendant, I started to think it was meant for Charlotte, especially after she said she grew up hanging out at the beach house with Jocelyn Forest. But then we found the king chess piece, and it's clearly a reference to the Forest's home on King Street. That takes us back to them. How long ago was Jocelyn married? I don't remember now."

"It's been several years now…three or four." Gloria smiled, seeming to reminisce as she let out a wistful sigh. "She made a beautiful bride."

"You don't think she's the target, do you? As the matron of honor?" I was struggling to make sense of all the clues we had gathered so far, and I was nervous we were going to miss something important. If another tragedy happened at the park—especially one we could have prevented—I'd never forgive myself. The pressure was beginning to feel like an elephant sitting on my chest.

Gloria sighed as she finished her second martini. "What we need is another clue…"

ZOE

I wanted to talk to Cat tonight, but she wasn't here. It was her night off. And also Gloria's night off. Why did I feel such a profound sense of…loss…knowing they weren't here?

The place just didn't feel right without them, and it made me think about when they were gone a while back. That was when Mr. Cool Cat went missing. Bad things happened when they were gone.

Well, bad things happened when they were here, too… I mean, the dead biped bodies and such. But at least when bad things happened when they were here, they helped. They knew what to do. I'd found I could trust them. Well, I couldn't communicate with Gloria like I could Cat, but if Cat trusted her, I knew I could too.

So, it probably shouldn't have surprised me that, when something bad happened, and she wasn't here to help me fix it, I panicked.

I was hunting while also keeping an eye and nose out for Mr. Cool Cat when Ice, Amber and Ziti ambushed me, flying out of the bushes like they were being chased by a rabid dog. Next thing I knew, they were surrounding me, panting and out of breath.

"What's going on?" I glanced from one pair of wild

glowing eyes to another as they attempted to catch their breath.

"It's Sass. She's sick. She ate a mouse behind the mushroom place, and it didn't agree with her." They were referring to one of the restaurants in the park.

"And that's an emergency?" My tail flicked back and forth as I waited for an explanation.

"You don't understand—she's like foaming at the mouth and wailing sick," Amber explained. "C'mon, you've gotta come see her. She asked for you."

"She did?" I could hardly believe that. Sass and I were barely civil to one another, and I'd caught her cavorting with Scar and his mob more than once.

"Please, Zoe, you have to believe us!" Ziti pleaded. "She might not make it."

"Okay, take me to her." I followed them on a long romp to Magical Mushroom Restaurant, my paws pounding against the cool, damp ground. It had rained earlier, and the smell of rain and fallen leaves was thick in the air.

We ran as fast as we could, but when we got there, a group of bipeds was swarming the spot where my fellow felines claimed they'd left Sass. Flashlight beams danced over the area, and one beam revealed a small plastic and wire carrier.

I motioned for the crew to hide out with me in the bushes several cat-lengths away. "I think they're trying to help her."

At least I hoped that was what I was seeing. I recognized The Wrangler. He was the one responsible for us. He was not a nice man. We all pretty much loathed him and tried to avoid him as much as possible. He was the one who took Moony away a while back when Scar and his goons got him into trouble.

"Will we ever see her again?" Ziti whispered when The Wrangler loaded the carrier into a motorized cart. He climbed in, along with the other bipeds, and they raced toward the back of the park.

"I don't know. I hope they're getting her help, and she'll be back. You said she ate a mouse and got sick?" I shuddered at the thought. What was wrong with that mouse?

"What seems to be the problem over here?" a familiar voice oozed like slime out of the bushes, getting louder as its owner approached. "Did you guys lose one of your clowder? Aw, what a shame!"

"Vinny," I sneered. "What are you doing over here?"

"Did they just take away one of your members?" He sat up straight under the light, the brightness illuminating the tuxedo pattern of his coat.

Two more of Scar's henchmen sauntered out of the bushes and took their spots on either side of Vinny, Scar's right-hand cat. "This one givin' ya problems, Boss?" the one said, his tail swishing aggressively back and forth behind him.

"Easy, Bruce. We're just here to find out what happened." Vinny turned back toward me. "Did they take one of your cats or what, Z?"

"They did. Sass," I answered, too worried to say something snarky to this meddling meat ax. "She got sick from eating a mouse. I guess it was pretty bad."

"It was terrible!" Ziti and Amber agreed in unison.

"She was foaming at the mouth," Ice added.

"Yeah," Vinny said in a rare conciliatory tone, "we had that happen a while back. Only they never brought him back to us."

"One of your clowder got sick from eating a mouse?" I clarified.

"That's right. He never came back. Pretty sure he spent his ninth life, ya know?"

"Sorry to hear that." And I truly was. None of us deserved

to go out that way. "Do we have any idea why the mouse made him sick?"

Vinny drew closer to me, a few steps away from his goons. They didn't follow. He leaned close to me. "Word on the street? It was poison."

I gasped, "Poison?"

I wasn't sure how Vinny knew that word. I only knew what poison was from watching all those crime shows with the Security bipeds back in the day. In those shows, whenever a female biped wanted to kill someone and do it on the downlow...they'd use poison. They'd sneak it into the victim's food or drink.

The folks at Fairytale Forest wanted us to eat the mice and other rodents in the park. That was our whole reason for being here. Our job. So I knew they wouldn't deliberately poison any of the mice. They wouldn't want us to get sick.

But what if someone else wanted us to?

Nine

We were driving off the peninsula and over the Ravenel Bridge so I could take Gloria home when I felt an odd sensation tugging at me. I couldn't quite tell if it was my head or my heart being yanked in the other direction—west—but, whatever it was, it was impossible to ignore.

"What's wrong?" Gloria seemed to pick up on my pensive vibe. "You're quiet, and you're hardly ever quiet."

"I need to go to the park," I said. "Something's not right."

"Right now, you got an urge to go to work? On our night off? Is it something you ate?" Gloria snickered.

I laughed too, but it was an uneasy chuckle. "No, the food at 82 Queen was phenomenal as always. You know I didn't have anything but the one cocktail—and holy cow it was good. But that was an hour ago now, and I just got this sinking feeling in my stomach that something is wrong."

Her brows furrowed when I glanced over at her. "And it's not the bourbon pecan pie?"

"I don't think so." This feeling emanated from deep in the pit of my gut—plus a little echo in my head and a pounding in my heart. My entire body was trying to tell me to turn around and go the other direction.

Gloria's voice took on a resolved tone. "Well, if you think you need to go to the park because something's wrong, turn around and take me with you."

"But don't you need to get home and get some rest?" I had planned to drop her at her house and then return to the park.

"Do I need to remind you that we are both creatures of the night? We're used to being awake all night long. We can sleep tomorrow during the day, like vampires." Her voice oozed like honey, and I didn't detect one bit of untruth in her words.

"Okay. Well, I've gotta get over the bridge first. Can't exactly turn around on it, ya know." I laughed and kept flying down the lower part heading into Mount Pleasant. At the first opportunity, I swung my Rogue into a parking lot and whipped it back around. Next thing I knew, we were flying back over the Ravenel and down US17 across the peninsula and historic district once more. At least at this time of night, there wasn't much traffic.

About fifteen minutes later, I was pulling into the employee parking lot at Fairytale Forest. We hustled through security and the employee gates, and next thing we knew, were stepping onto Storybook Street just as the crowds were pushing their way toward the exits.

"I feel like a fish swimmin' upstream!" Gloria complained as we waded through the crowds.

Something inside me was directing me toward the bushes where Zoe and her clowder lived. With the guests leaving the park, I might have a chance to speak to her and find out what happened.

And I knew something happened; I just didn't know what. I hoped it wasn't a dead body.

But I had a bad feeling.

"Zoe," I whispered, "if you can hear me, meet me at the castle as soon as you can."

All I received for confirmation was a pair of glowing green eyes blinking back within the dark recesses of the shrubbery. I turned to Gloria. "C'mon, let's head over. She'll be there, I'm sure."

Gloria didn't question me, and we took the path past the tree and Dragon's Lair Pizza, over to the castle, where Zoe and I often met. Hardly anyone was ever there at night, and though the custodians maintained the nearby restrooms, the inside of the castle was only cleaned early in the morning before guests arrived, usually by the day shift after we left the park.

We both took a seat on one of the benches in the atrium of the castle. An intricately woven tapestry of a field full of unicorns and lions with a forest behind them filled the wall across from us. I was marveling at the tiny flowers in white, yellow and red, and how they contrasted with the various shades of green making up the background when a ruckus of cats burst onto the scene—Zoe and two of her comrades, one gray tabby and one light yellow—Ziti and Amber, if I wasn't mistaken.

"Cat! Cat!" She skittered to a stop right in front of me. "Didn't think you were here tonight. Something's happened to Sass. She got sick, and they took her away, and Vinny said something about poison and—"

"Whoa, dumplin'," I held a hand up to hopefully get her to stop and breathe, "bless your heart. Relax a sec and tell me what happened—slower this time."

Her fluffy gray fur was tufted along her back, and her tail looked like a plume as she tried to compose herself. Eyes wide with terror, she licked her lips once before starting over. "Sass got sick, and The Wrangler and his assistants took her away in one of those traps like they took Moony in. And then Vinny showed up and said one of their clowder members got sick not long ago and…died." She looked down at the floor as her tail swished back and forth.

"Oh no! See, I thought something was wrong, didn't I, Gloria? She said a couple cats have gotten sick, and one died." I looked over at my friend, and she nodded solemnly, putting a hand on my shoulder for support. "What can I do, Zoe?"

I'd never seen her look so desperate, so vulnerable. "Can you talk to The Wrangler? Find out where they took her? If she's going to be okay? If she's coming back?"

I stood up, taking a deep breath as my entire being filled with resolve. As much as Zoe had done for me, the least I could do was help her find out about her friend. "Which one is Sass again? I can't exactly tell Sam that you asked for my help."

"Right. She's a pure-black shorthair with wiry, slim build. Slinky. Like that giant pretend cat they have displayed as part of the…decorations." She enunciated the word in a way that made me smile. Cats probably did think all of our human holidays and their traditions were strange, didn't they?

"Okay, got it. We'll go talk to Sam now." I looked toward Gloria, who nodded in agreement. "We'll come find you if we can learn any information."

"Thank you so much, Cat. Thank you." Her pleading green eyes blinked twice, and then she and her cohort skedaddled.

"Well, gonna fill me on the way to talk to Sam?" Gloria asked. Sometimes I forgot that she couldn't hear Zoe—only I could. So I had to repeat the conversation as we walked back to the tree.

"Sam? You down here?" I called down the stairs. It

seemed…creepier and darker down there than I remembered. There was a single fluorescent light bulb casting a greenish-white glow over white walls and stainless-steel fixtures.

"Come on down," his voice reverberated up the tunnel that was the stairwell.

Gloria gave me a look that said she wasn't sure if she wanted to go down there.

"You wanna wait for me outside?" I checked.

She rolled her eyes. "In for a penny, in for a pound," she answered.

"Is that Gullah wisdom?" I teased her.

"Nope, I think it's Dickens," she said with a grin.

We made it down the stairs and took in the sight of multiple cages stacked from floor to ceiling to house cats. Newcomers to the clowders in the park were quarantined here while they had shots and other tests run. They were also spayed or neutered so we didn't have dozens of litters of kittens every year. Though, the thought of seeing tiny little kittens prowling around the park sure did make my heart go pitter-patter. Every once in a while, a pregnant cat was brought in, and then we did have kittens, but it had been a long while since that happened. Zoe came from one of the last litters I remembered being born in the park, so she had always been here.

"What can I do for you, ladies?" Sam enquired as he emerged from a large walk-in supplies closet.

"Hi, Sam. Did you take a black female shorthair from the courtyard clowder this evening?" I got straight to the point.

"Oh, yeah, that's the little mollie I pulled out from behind the Magical Mushroom Restaurant, ain't it? She wasn't doing too good. Took her straight to the cat hospital up on 61 in West Ashley. They're gonna call after they examine her," he explained.

"I heard another cat was poisoned a few nights ago," I continued my hunt for intel. "Do you know anything about that?"

"Well, not yet." He didn't seem suspicious about me asking so many questions, surprisingly enough. "They're doing a necropsy. We wanna make sure it's not something contagious."

"You didn't quarantine those two cats?" I probed. Zoe would be proud.

"Well, now, I thought about it, but the clowders have been mixing more than ever—sometimes getting into fights. It's impossible to trace exposure. I'd have to practically quarantine the whole lot of 'em." Right as he finished explaining, a landline phone attached to the wall near the closet rang. "Excuse me a sec, ladies."

He stepped over and answered the phone. "Uh-huh. Okay. And what's the prognosis? Okay. Yeah, sure. No problem. Yep, will do."

He hung up and stepped back over to us, wiping his hands on his navy uniform work pants. "Well, that was the hospital. Sounds like we got the mollie there in time. They pumped her belly and found the remains of a rodent—they're gonna test it for poisons. The other cat I took there yesterday—same thing. They're running tests for him too." He took a deep breath as if it was sinking in that he lost one cat and might have lost two others had he not gotten them to the doctor in time.

He scratched his head. "Sure hope there's nothing out there that's gonna hurt any more cats."

"Me too," I agreed, and Gloria touched my arm, nodding.

"What can we do?" she asked. "Anything to help? We're here at night and often see the cats about."

"Right. Well, you two are those detective chicks, ain't ya? The ones who solved the two murders in the park?" The last part of his sentence was whispered, even though there was no one around but us.

I nodded. "Well, we helped figure out the murderers, yes. Only one of them was done in the park though. The other body being found here was just a coincidence."

That was what I wanted to believe, but, honestly, I wasn't so sure. Was someone targeting the cats now?

"No one at the park is using poison on the rodents," he said. "So that's not the problem. They know better than that. But there are plenty of toxic substances rodents could get into, and they might make cats sick if they eat them. Could you two keep an eye out? Just, you know, if anything looks funny?"

I nodded. Seemed everyone wanted us to "keep an eye out" these days. "We do tend to notice things that others don't. We have an eye for detail." When I glanced over at Gloria, she smiled.

"Will you let us know what you find out about the cats?" Gloria asked.

"Of course. Will do. I know y'all care about them as much as I do." His mouth turned up at the corners into what was a smile for him. "Thanks for checking on Sass."

"Of course, Sam. Thanks for taking care of them." We headed back up the stairs and into the night.

"Poison." Gloria shuddered. "After hearing on the carriage tour that Harriet Mackie, the Dead Bride, was poisoned, and now some of the cats have been too—it makes me not want to eat or drink anything."

"Good thing we had a nice big poison-free dinner at 82 Queen. We won't need to eat for a while." I looked at the stars swirling in a light haze of clouds. "But this issue with the cats...it can't possibly be related to what's going on with Charlotte's wedding, right?"

Gloria shrugged. "I sure as heck hope not."

ZOE

Cat met up with me later in the night to let me know she'd talked to The Wrangler, and Sass was going to be okay. They were going to keep her at the hospital for a while so she could recover. But Cat also confirmed they suspected the mouse she ate was poisoned, and they were checking that and the poison that killed Scar's goon to see if they were the same.

So...now Cool was still missing, and Sass had been poisoned.

Things were not going well.

I needed to rally the troops. Bipeds used the expression "herding cats" to describe getting difficult bipeds to align and work together, and I felt that with every fiber of my being. It was not going to be easy. But I had to try.

Moony summoned everyone for me, and soon I was looking out at the wary eyes of my clowder: Moony and Snow were closest to me; then Ziti, Amber, and Ice made up the second row; with Daisy, Priss and Hank in the back. Hank was snoozing, but I hissed at him until he woke up.

"Look, I need everyone paying attention to me." Ears perked up as eyes drilled into mine, unblinking. "Good, listen, Sass was taken to the hospital, and she should be okay, but she did get sick from eating a mouse. One of Scar's thugs apparently also ate a tainted mouse, but he didn't make it—"

A choked gasp came out of Princess's mouth, then Daisy nearly fainted. *Drama queens. Every clowder has them.*

"Buck up, soldiers, we need to be extra vigilant. I'm

worried perhaps Cool got ahold of one too, and maybe he didn't make it either."

There was a melancholy silence as everyone contemplated my theory.

"I don't want anyone else to get sick, so I need you to be super-duper observant of your prey. No chasing a rodent that is lethargic or acts sick. Only pursue a mouse that gives chase and seems healthy. DO NOT, under any circumstances, consume a creature that is already dead. That's ick anyway—we're not scavengers. Hank, are you listening? I'm talking specifically to you, buddy."

He lifted his head, looking perturbed that I'd called him out. "Fine, Zoe."

"And I'm going to be checking in with the other clowders we don't see much—like the ones out by the rollercoasters—to see if anyone has seen Mr. Cool Cat and to warn them about the tainted mice." Then, to myself, I mumbled, "I should have had Cat ask The Wrangler about him too. Drat…"

Snow looked at me and raised a paw. "Sorry for the interruption, Zoe, and this is probably not what you want to hear, but…" There was an almost tender look in his gaze.

"What?" I prompted him. "You don't need to beat around the bush. Just tell me."

"I think you're going to need to accept that Cool is gone. He was an old man." His tone became infuriatingly patronizing. "He wasn't going to survive out there long on his own."

My nostrils flared as I looked at my new friend, who had only known me, Cool and the rest of the gang for a short time. "Mr. Cool Cat is extremely wise and resourceful. If anyone could navigate this park on their own, it's him. He's probably just hiding out until he feels better. Or maybe he's been feeling ill and is worried about bringing something contagious back to the clowder. Cool was a brave warrior in his day. He will be back soon. I can feel it."

No one else argued with me, but Snow approached, tapping his paw against mine affectionately. His tail brushed against mine as his eyes locked onto me. "I just don't want you to get your hopes up, Zoe."

I understood where he was coming from, but he didn't know Mr. Cool Cat like I did. Not to mention he had this air of superiority, like I was just this silly little molly who didn't know my tail from a hole in the ground. Was he really cavorting with Vinny and the rest of Scar's thugs?

"We don't know if what's happening to the mice and cats in the park is related to the dead biped bodies showing up," I continued, ignoring Snow's statement. "It's possible this is a targeted attack. We must be vigilant. Do not let your guard down. I also wouldn't be surprised if Scar and his mob have something to do with this."

I zoned in on Snow to see if he reacted to my accusation and witnessed the very slightest ear twitch. *Interesting*.

Ziti piped up, "You think they're involved, even though they lost a member?"

"I wouldn't put anything past him. You know he's likely seeking revenge for what we helped the River Cats do to him."

Snow had been in on that glorious triumph and absolutely reveled in embarrassing the fur off of Scar and Vinny. I thought he was going to be loyal to me and to my clowder. But now I was definitely questioning his allegiance.

Everyone looked appropriately serious and concerned. *Good*. I didn't want my clowder to be scared, but a healthy dose of fear could help keep everyone safe. I was their leader, and keeping them safe was my job.

I just hoped I hadn't failed Cool or Sass.

Ten

"**D**id you get any sleep last night?" I asked Gloria on our way into the city. My Rogue was earning its keep, transporting me over to Mt. Pleasant and then into the Charleston historic district so many times this week.

"A little. I'm…nervous. You know, I've been thinking about what's going on, and I decided this is more nerve-racking than investigating a murder," Gloria shared.

"Oh, yeah? Why is that?"

"Because when you're investigating a murder, it's already happened. There's no onus to prevent it. Right now, I'm feeling a lot of pressure to prevent Charlotte from being hurt," she explained.

I kept my eyes on the road as I considered her statement. "That makes sense. I just can't decide if someone's messing with us, or if she's really in danger."

"Considering what's already happened in the park the last few months, I think we have to assume she is in danger."

Gloria sighed and turned to look out the window at the passing scenery.

I nodded. "But we didn't get any warnings before, and I'm still not convinced all these clues we're getting now are related to the other two murders. And I have no clue how the other two would be related to each other, but I will tell you one thing…"

"What's that?" Gloria's eyebrow arched.

"It's driving me absolutely crazy not being able to figure it out. I didn't get much sleep at all last night, for the record," I confessed. "I was mulling all of these clues over, along with the other two murders, and I just can't make any connections. Except for all the connections to the park. That's the only commonality."

"Well," Gloria sighed again, obviously sharing my frustration, "let's just focus on keeping Charlotte safe for now. Isn't that all we can do? Maybe we will get answers about how it connects to the other incidents—if it connects at all—after the wedding."

"Right," I agreed.

It was early, just after eight o'clock, and I managed to find a parking space very close to the South Carolina Society Hall where Marci worked. It must have been some sort of parking miracle. Society Hall was a white building with classic columns supporting the second floor and roof, with a large balcony overlooking Meeting Street.

The traditional design continued inside with elegant fixtures and woodwork. "Now, why wouldn't Charlotte want to get married in St. Michael's with the reception here? It's so much prettier and classier than getting married in a fake graveyard in a theme park," Gloria announced as she looked around the impressively appointed lobby.

"Are you looking to host an event?" came a voice from an antique oak desk just feet away from a beautiful fireplace.

The voice belonged to a petite white woman with auburn hair neatly coiled on top of her head. She had pale skin and wore tortoiseshell glasses.

"No, no, we're actually looking for someone who works here. Marci Beauchamp?" I asked in my warmest, friendliest voice. "Do you know where we could find her?"

"One moment please," the woman said curtly, her smile disappearing. She depressed a button on her phone and said something in a low voice into the receiver. She paused for a moment, then returned the receiver to its cradle. "Second floor, third door on the left."

"Oh, thank you." I smiled and turned to Gloria, who also smiled at the receptionist and expressed her thanks.

We headed up the stairs, fingers trailing along the wrought-iron railing. "That was easier than I expected," I murmured as we reached the top and headed toward the third door on the left.

"She didn't seem to like the fact that we wanted to see Marci though. She was friendly until you said that name."

"Maybe it's because we don't want to host an event?" I suggested. "Maybe they work on commission. Could be why Marci is upset Charlotte doesn't want to host her reception here."

"Could be." Gloria stepped forward and knocked on the door, which was only open a crack.

"Come in, come in," Marci invited us inside.

We pushed open the tall, heavy door to reveal her perched on her desk chair, this time wearing a frilly yellow dress with daisies embroidered on the yoke. Why did this grown woman dress like an American Girl doll?

"Hi, Marci, I'm sure you remember us from Charlotte's office a couple of days ago. I'm—"

"Catherine Lyon, and you're Gloria Bress. I remember." Her tone was not snippy, just matter-of-fact. "Have a seat.

My apologies for insisting you leave my client's office so abruptly."

We both sat in pale-green wingback chairs opposite her desk, which also looked antique but was walnut instead of oak like the one in the lobby. There was a clipboard resting on the surface holding a program for an event hosted by the Charleston Players. I assumed it was some sort of theatre troupe.

"I appreciate that," I said. "We're only trying to help."

"Charlotte is…" Marci sucked in a deep breath as she moved the clipboard to a drawer in the desk. Her chest visibly expanded, moving the daisy appliques on her dress up and down as she relaxed again. "She is battling a lot of anxiety about the wedding, and she doesn't always deal with situations in a level-headed manner."

Hmm. I didn't get that impression from her when we were in her office, but I was going to let Marci speak her mind. Maybe we'd learn something valuable for our investigation… if that was what we were calling it.

"She is about two situations away from losing it," Marci continued, "so I needed to intervene. After your visit, her daddy told her some of the stuff that's been going on in the park, and it took about a half-gallon of Ben & Jerry's and a Xanax to calm her down. We have to get her to the altar in one piece on Saturday."

I smiled. Mr. Carson didn't say anything about his daughter's anxiety either, so this was all unexpected information. "I'm glad she has you to keep her steady."

Marci beamed. "Yes, she and I have been through a lot together, that's for sure. Bless her heart."

Gloria's gaze shifted from Marci to me, so fast I'm sure the younger woman didn't notice. But I knew how to interpret that darting glance, and it undoubtedly conveyed, *I don't believe one word of this hogwash, and I'm gonna let you handle it from here.*

I wanted to be strategic—didn't want to waste our time or Marci's. "She's lucky to have you as a friend. What can we do to help the wedding day go smoothly?"

"I appreciate y'all's help," Marci said, fluttering her thick eyelashes at us, "but between Jocelyn, myself, and the other bridesmaids, I'm sure we have it under control. I'm just hoping Walker and Kenny don't pull any shenanigans."

I leaned toward her desk. "What kind of shenanigans?"

Marci sighed. "Well, you may have heard that Walker is the one insisting on having the wedding at the park. His best man, Kenny Davenport, works there as the head of landscaping. Now there's a bit of drama between them with Kenny's girlfriend, Ellie, but that's over now."

"What kind of drama?"

She waved away my question. "Walker used to date Ellie before he met Charlotte, and, when he dumped Ellie, she started dating Kenny, so it's all good now, but…" She let out a long, exasperated sigh like she was over all the drama. "Ellie and Charlotte used to be friends too, and, well, you know how girls are…"

I raised an eyebrow. "I guess I don't. I have two sons…and I wasn't…well, I didn't have a group of catty girlfriends when I was growing up," I explained.

"Well, I'm not worried about Ellie. She's moved up to Clemson anyway to start grad school. It's the guys pulling something that I'm scared of." She rolled her eyes.

I leaned closer to her as if discussing a top secret, something super classified. "What do you think they'd pull?"

"The other stuff you've found so far? The bouquet and the locket?" Marci rolled her eyes again for good measure. "Wouldn't be surprised if Kenny was behind it. Or even Walker. They are completely nuts when they get together."

"Like nuts how?" I probed a little deeper.

"Oh, they're always pulling silly pranks. Like, one time Kenny got Charlotte's keys from Walker and moved her car when they were at some event, and when she came out, she couldn't find her car until Walker finally cracked up laughing and told her what was going on."

"Wow, that's childish," I agreed. "And she wants to marry him?"

Marci picked at her cuticle. "Yup, though most of the time it's all Kenny's idea. Walker just rolls with it."

"Oh, that reminds me, we did find another odd thing after we spoke with you the other day," I shared.

Her eyebrows, a few shades darker than her hair and a lot thicker than what used to be fashionable, rose. "And what was that?"

I wished I'd brought the piece of evidence to show her, but I'd left it with Mr. Forest and Mr. Carson. "It was a chess piece—the king—and it was left on one of the gravestones in the area where the wedding is going to take place."

"Oh, a chess piece." She laughed and waved her hand again dismissively. "Kenny is like a chess master."

"He is?" That didn't sound like someone who was a jokester and prankster. Chess seemed like such a stuffy...sport... if you wanted to call it that.

"Oh, yeah, that sounds just like Kenny." She nodded repeatedly. "He was probably leaving it as a calling card."

"So, the chess piece had a tiny owl on the bottom and the number of the Forests' house on King Street. Their front door has a statue of an owl above it."

"Oh, yes, Hooter—I'm familiar." She laughed like it was just another big joke. "That's what Jamie and the guys call it. That definitely sounds like something Kenny would do. You know, when we spoke the other day, I thought perhaps they were involved, but I figured that would upset Charlotte even more, so I didn't mention it. Kenny is probably trying to get Walker all riled up."

"So you really think this is all Kenny and Walker, then. You don't think it's someone actually out to hurt Charlotte?" I asked. "How would Walker even know what's going on, since he doesn't work there?"

"Through Charlotte," Marci explained. "Trust me, this is all very on-brand for them."

"So you don't think there's any actual threat to Charlotte?" Gloria chimed in.

She sighed and shook her head. "Nah. I mean, Charlotte is a good person, very sweet girl, kind, easy to be around. It was hard sometimes being her friend in college because people just flock to her. She's gorgeous and smart too. Kinda unfair, if ya think about it. We both pledged the same sorority at C of C—she got in, and I didn't. That stung, ya know, but I got over it. She isn't the one who didn't choose me. Well, I mean, she didn't choose me to be her maid of honor—she chose Jocie. But she and Jocie have known each other longer, since they were kids, on account of their dads being BFFs, so that makes sense. And because Walker wants to get married at the park, so it makes sense."

She kept saying that…"it makes sense." But did it? She didn't seem concerned at all that someone might actually be out to get her client. I sure hoped she was correct.

"What about Jocelyn?" I asked next. "You don't think she has any enemies, do you? Is she kind and sweet like Charlotte is?"

Marci's face screwed up for a moment like she was surprised by my question and needed a moment to think about it. In the few seconds of silence that ensued, I checked in with Gloria, whose arched eyebrows told me she was also surprised by my question. But if Charlotte didn't have any enemies…maybe the Forests did. Maybe that was why this stuff kept happening in the park. Gloria and I had discussed the possibility this was all connected, but we just couldn't identify a common thread. Perhaps it was someone with a vendetta against the Forests.

Plus, I still wasn't sure the bouquet showing up at the Forests' beach house and the king chess piece having their house number on it was aimed at Charlotte.

"So, Jocelyn Forest Whitaker…" Marci steepled her hands before interlacing her fingers and resting her elbows on her desk. "She is an interesting character. The middle child—or so they want you to think."

"What do you mean by that?"

"Well, not very many people know this, but Jamie Forest isn't actually Janelle's kid," Marci shared.

"What?" Gloria and I both exclaimed in unison, looking at each other with wide eyes and open mouths.

Marci laughed. "Yeah, guess that news hasn't made it around the Fairytale Forest workforce, has it?" She bent her fingers back now, making her knuckles crack loudly. "Mr. Forest had an affair early on in his marriage—and his mistress conceived Jamison. He paid her off, and Janelle has raised him as her own son."

"Wow…" I blinked several times in rapid succession. "That is…wow." The Forests were the epitome of Family Values. It was hard to believe—

"The Forests have plenty of enemies," Marci continued blowing our minds. "There are a number of politicians, not to mention other businesspeople they stepped on to get to where they are in life. Now, are they wildly popular in Charleston and the surrounding areas? Yes. Everyone likes the revenue they bring to the Low Country. But…mark my words, they have enemies."

I tried to reconcile everything she'd just shared with what I knew of my employers. "So you don't think the bouquet that was delivered to their beach house, and the chess piece… you don't think they were sent to warn the Forests of something else happening in their park?"

"Nah, I still think that's all Kenny Davenport. He works at the park. He has access—especially to flowers and chess pieces. He probably even knows about your little detective side gigs." She gestured at Gloria and me. "He's a smart guy. He's probably just messing with Charlotte and Walker."

I was starting to feel like our next interview should be with Kenny Davenport. I appreciated how honest and forthcoming Marci had been. Plus, she was correct: access to the park was a definite factor. She didn't have the kind of access Kenny did. I was fairly certain we could cross her off our list of suspects. Yes, she harbored some envy of the bride. But she was a businesswoman, and I didn't think she'd want to jeopardize her business by playing games with one of her clients.

"Thanks for sharing your insights with us." I reached out to shake Marci's hand. "Please let us know if there's anything we can do to help make Charlotte's wedding day run smoothly."

"If you talk to Kenny just…well…tell him to back off," Marci suggested. "That'll help both me and Charlotte."

ZOE

"Why do we keep coming back here?" Amber asked as I herded my clowder into the woods. I was once again reminded of the "herding cats" idiom. I'd have to say the bipeds completely nailed it on that one.

"Because something isn't right in here, and I feel like it

has something to do with Mr. Cool Cat," I said for approximately the four millionth time. *Cats can't count, ya know.*

This time I had Ziti, Moony, Ice, and Snow with me, along with Amber. All of my strongest and best warriors were by my side.

"Look at the fog rising from those stones." Moony shivered as he stopped in his tracks and lifted his head toward the sky. He sniffed twice at the air, then down at the ground.

"You look like a dog," I told him as I came up behind him.

"It smells weird here," was his only explanation.

Every time I came here, something was new. The bipeds had been doing a lot of work in this area of the park. First they hung all the tiny lights in the trees, then they put up these stone things, and now there was a huge archway covered in leaves, sticks, flowers, and other weird-looking biped stuff. Bipeds and their "decorations"—geez.

"What are these big round things everywhere? They're creepy," Ziti said, circling one on a stone step that led up to a big slab of stone in the shape of a box. Cats are generally fans of boxes, but this one was too big and too cold.

"Those are pumpkins," I explained. "They're actually fruits. Bipeds associate them with their celebration called Halloween."

"Hallowhat?" Ice asked.

Snow gave a smug smirk. "Oh, yes. My previous associate was a fan of Halloween. I remember now. He also put up decorations that involved similar motifs to what we see here. Skeletons. Witches. Pumpkins. Graveyards."

"Graveyards?" Moony's ears twitched. "What's that?"

"You're standing in one," Snow announced. "It's not a real one, but still. It's meant to look like one."

"What's a real one? What's the difference?" Ice prodded.

Snow seemed to be an expert in this department. "It's

where bipeds bury their dead and stick a stone to mark the spot where they're buried."

"Ewww, dead bodies? Buried in the ground?" It was Ziti's turn to shudder.

"That's correct. These are just for fun though." Snow looked even smugger than usual.

"That doesn't sound fun to me at all," Amber contributed.

"Hey, I don't remember these being here before." I sauntered over to one end of the huge box, circling a tall stone pot filled with a bush that was heavy with berries.

"Oh, don't eat those! Don't even touch them," Snow said once he joined me.

"What are they?" I started to ask, but then my brother raced past me.

Moony sniffed around the pot. "Oh, man! Look down here." He gestured with his head toward something partially hidden by the vine-flower-arch-thingie.

Then I caught a whiff of death and decay. My first thought was…Mr. Cool Cat.

Worry shooting through me, I tentatively moved closer to where my brother was investigating. "What is it?"

His head popped back up. "Two dead rats."

"Did someone say rats?" Ice's ears perked up.

"No!" I blocked Ice's path. "What did I say about eating anything questionable? Two dead rats are questionable." I turned back to Snow. "Now, what were you going to say about these berries in the pots?"

"They're poison," he said matter-of-factly. "My associate had an interest in toxic and poisonous plants and animals. We watched a number of documentaries on the television. I remember seeing those—can't remember what they're called though. If those rats ate the berries, that's what killed them."

"But they smell good," Ice insisted.

Moony shook his head. "The rats? Eww. They're rotting."

"No, the berries." Ice moved closer, licking his lips. "Don't you ever get a hankering for a plant? Grass or weeds or flowers? Those berries look tantalizing."

I shoved him back. "No, Ice. They're poison."

"They might have smelled good to the rats too. They're even more opportunistic than we are," Snow theorized. "Actually—that could be what the mice ate, the ones that killed Klaus and made Sass sick."

"Wait…did you say Klaus?" I stared at him, unblinking.

"He was part of Scar's gang," Snow explained.

I never told anyone the name of Scar's thug who died. How did Snow know?

I'd have to worry about that later. Right now, the berries needed to be dealt with. "I have to tell Cat. This is where that wedding celebration is going to take place. She should know there's something dangerous here."

"Well, bipeds should know they're poisonous and not to eat them," Snow said. "If they watched the same documentary Kevin and I watched, they'd know—"

"I'm going to tell her anyway," I insisted. She told me to tell her about anything out of the ordinary I came across in the park, and maybe she could find out if this plant was what indirectly made Sass sick.

"Hey, there's something else back here too." Moony poked his head back behind the archway again. I hoped he wasn't getting too close to the dead rats. But he emerged a second later with a small book in his mouth.

"I wonder what that is?" Ziti sniffed it as he dropped it at my feet.

"I can't read the writing, but Cat will be able to," I said confidently. "C'mon, guys, let's check the whole area for Cool. And then I can go track down Cat."

Eleven

CATHERINE

We came in early to meet with Mr. Forest and Mr. Carson again to give them updates about what we'd found so far. I mentioned the sick cat, and Mr. Forest said he'd check into it, but he doubted it was related. I didn't tell them about our meeting with Marci or what I'd learned about Mr. Forest's son, Jamison. I was just going to file that last tidbit away.

What I did tell them was that we'd heard the best man, who also worked here in the park as the head of landscaping, was a bit of a practical joker.

"It's true, Kenny has a wicked sense of humor," Mr. Carson agreed. "It's like he lives for April Fool's Day, you know? If I find out he's the one messing with Charlotte, though, he's not gonna like my response."

Mr. Forest backed him up. "His job is going to be in jeopardy if I find out he has anything to do with this."

I hoped for Kenny's sake that he didn't, but that would sure make our investigation that much easier, wouldn't it?

When Mr. Carson said he had a "wicked" sense of humor, maybe he meant that more literally…

"We also heard Kenny is a chess champion," I relayed. "And that may explain the king chess piece."

"He better not be the one behind that." Mr. Forest shook his fist for emphasis. I hadn't seen him that angry for a long time. Not since one of the rides broke down, and he couldn't get the parts needed to fix it for a month. "I know he's mad about all the work we gave his crew for the Haunted Wood area where the wedding is going to take place, but surely he wouldn't be so childish."

"Surely," I agreed. "But we're going to talk to him anyway. If that's okay with you?"

"He comes in early," Mr. Carson, who was his direct boss as the operations manager, informed us. "So he should be in his office before you leave at the end of your shift."

"Great, thanks!"

Gloria and I barely made it out of the facility services building before Zoe appeared with something in her mouth. She dropped it at my feet and scurried behind one of the dumpsters since someone was coming out of the building after us. It was a very small blue cloth-bound book with faded gold printing on the front and spine. It had a library classification sticker on the spine, and the pages were stamped "Addlestone Library – College of Charleston."

"What is it? A book?" Gloria crowded around me to get a look.

"Yes, hold on, the title is so faded, I can't read it. I need more light."

"Use your phone flashlight," Gloria recommended.

"Oh, right." I pulled it out of my fanny pack and shined the beam on the spine, where the printing was a hair more legible than the front. "The North American Guide to Poisonous Plants and Mushrooms," I read.

"Wow!" Gloria stepped back, her mouth gaping open. "I wonder where she found it?"

"Let's go to the castle. Hopefully she will meet us there." I threw my voice toward the dumpster, hoping she was still there, waiting for the coast to be clear.

We left our carts in a secure location and headed over to the castle near the river. "Funny, seems like we were just here, doesn't it?"

"We have been seeing Zoe a lot," Gloria agreed. "I'm glad we have her help."

"Not sure what we'd do without her, to be honest. Never thought I'd be relying on a cat so much—I never even thought cats were reliable." I still had no clue where my ability to communicate with her came from. I had owned cats off and on my entire life, and none of those cats could speak to me. I definitely needed to get my head checked—if I could ever find the time. I was being run ragged investigating mysteries!

I really deserved a raise. As did Gloria.

"I think Zoe is just one of a kind," Gloria said with an amused smirk. She patted the colorful scarf she wore tonight. "The wind is picking up—I think it might rain. All my joints are starting to ache."

"Great, that will make for a fun night. We shoulda grabbed some ponchos and umbrellas when we clocked in and picked up our carts."

Before she could respond, we heard the scampering of paws on the tile floor. Zoe appeared around the corner—alone this time, which surprised me. She almost always had an entourage.

"Everyone else is looking for Mr. Cool Cat. Have you heard anything else about Sass? Is she coming back?" Her bright green eyes held a plea.

"I haven't had a chance to talk to Sam yet. We just clocked

in," I said. "Most everyone is on Storybook Street for the closing show and will probably be there when you make your way back, so you need to be careful."

"I will," she agreed.

"Tell me about this book you brought us." I held it up. It was a little too big to fit in my fanny pack, so I'd tucked it in the waistband of my leggings, and fortunately my oversized cardigan covered it.

"We were looking for Mr. Cool Cat in the woods where you said the wedding is going to be. First off, we found some dead rats. Snow thought they'd eaten some poisonous berries that showed up in big pots near the arching vine thingie."

I looked over at Gloria and filled her in. "Poisonous berries in the wedding area!"

"The book!" she gasped.

"Exactly." I turned back to Zoe. "Do you think you could show us these plants tonight?"

"You can't miss them. They're in two huge pots on either side of that big stone box."

"The altar?" I confirmed.

She walked in a circle before sitting down, her fluffy tail curling around her long gray fur. "If that's what it's called. I told my cats not to eat any of the berries, or any rodents that might have sampled them."

"Good call. We've already decided to look up the head landscaper when he gets in in the morning. But we're gonna go check out the pots now. Well, as soon as the park clears out."

Gloria laughed. "Guess that means we should go do some work in the meantime. Do you want the men's restroom or women's?"

I rolled my eyes. "You know the women's is the worst..."

GLORIA WAS RIGHT ABOUT THE RAIN. A MISTY, DRIZZLY SHOWER started up as soon as we were done in the bathrooms near the courtyard. We ran into the facility services building to get ponchos and umbrellas, and I grabbed some flashlights too so we could head over to the Haunted Wood.

"And where do you two think you're going?" Sheri's voice called down the hallway, freezing us in our tracks.

"Uh…we're on a special assignment from Mr. Forest," I reminded her. "At least until the wedding is over."

"You two have barely accomplished anything beyond cleaning the courtyard bathrooms all week," she griped. "I'm glad the wedding is on Saturday so I can get my employees back."

"Well, it's better than having the park closed due to a murder," I snapped before we continued down the hallway and out the door into the worsening rain.

"How dare she get on our case when the owner of the whole park gave us a duty!" I snarled as we opened the umbrellas, trying to balance them as we also pushed the carts toward the Haunted Wood.

Gloria mused, "A mule that chews up his own collar is fixin' for a sore shoulder."

"Are you calling our boss a mule?" I snickered.

She laughed so hard, she slapped her knee. "Let's leave the carts here. Ms. Sheri can kiss my bootay!"

I sighed. "I miss Jayden being here—he would report her snarky comment to his dad, you know." The youngest Forest kiddo had spent the summer working with us, but he had left for College of Charleston in late August.

"Hey, speaking of Jayden, he might be able to help us

figure out how that book got here," Gloria suggested. "Sounds like it came from his college library."

"Good call. Maybe we can pay him a visit tomorrow. I'd like to know who checked it out. It can't be a coincidence that a book on poisonous plants shows up at the same time and place as poisonous berries, right?"

"Right…I wonder if it was left on purpose, like the necklace and the chess piece. It sounds like the poisonous berries are what is affecting the mice and also the cats—so they are all probably related after all," Gloria surmised.

"Why would that landscaper put out a poisonous plant knowing we have a cat population here in the park? It makes me so angry! I can't wait to talk to him in the morning. He's got a lot of explaining to do."

"Exactly."

We unlocked the gates to the Haunted Wood and saw that even more work had been done for the upcoming nuptials. The place looked so creepy in the mist rising up from the warm ground to hover around the fake gravestones. I shivered. "Let's get a look at these plants, take a picture of them, and get the heck out of Dodge!" I suggested.

"Good thinkin', my friend." Gloria nudged me with her shoulder as we both took cautious steps toward the altar and archway where Charlotte and Walker would be married in just a few days.

"Oh, here they are. Zoe was right—giant pots. They look like stone urns. And, yes, look at these berries! They look kinda like blueberries." I took my phone out of my fanny pack, holding it in one hand and my umbrella in the other as I made sure the flash was on and snapped a few quick pics.

Just as I was taking the second or third picture, we heard a shriek and then a wailing, tremulous voice, "Where is he? Where is my groom?"

Every single hair on my entire body stood on end as my

blood froze in my veins. Gloria reached out and grabbed my wrist as our eyes bolted across the graveyard, landing on a silvery-looking figure of a woman in a long white dress, seeming to hover above the mist.

Slowly she moved toward us with what looked like a teacup in her hand. "You're next," she cried, the sound echoing across the twenty or thirty yards that separated us from her. "You're next!"

"Run!" Gloria shouted. "Run, Cat!"

I finally got the message to travel from my brain to my legs, setting me in motion. Gloria jerked my arm hard, and I dropped the umbrella but managed to stuff my phone back into my pocket as we bolted for the gate. I fumbled with the keycard, my heart pounding against my ribcage like it might explode until I was able to scan it open.

We both ran out into the main part of the park, our eyes wide with terror, our hearts thumping, and our breaths coming in ragged gasps.

"She…was…wearing…a…wedding…dress…" was all Gloria could get out of her mouth before lightning streaked across the sky, casting the Haunted Wood in stark relief.

Before I could catch my breath, thunder rumbled throughout the clouds. The heavens opened up, releasing torrents of rain down upon us as we sank to our shaking-like-Jello knees, feeling like we were about to be swallowed up by the earth.

Twelve

When I saw two biped figures slumped on the ground in the pouring rain, I panicked. I recognized Cat and Gloria by what they were wearing earlier. Were they the next two biped bodies to be found dead in Fairytale Forest?

I ran like a rabid dog was chasing me to their side, relieved when I heard one of them groan. As a typical cat, I absolutely loathe getting wet. And, at this moment, I was getting drenched. That might be somewhat of a sign as to the depth of my feelings for these bipeds.

I let out a screech that was both ear-piercing and blood-curdling. The idea was to alert any felines or bipeds in the area that someone needed help—NOW.

I was relieved when I heard the ground shake as heavy, solid boots thundered across the muddy grass toward us. I knew from the smell before I could see that it was The Wrangler. I did not want him to know I was protecting bipeds, so I scurried away, hopeful he would get Cat and Gloria somewhere safe, warm, and dry.

I hid in the bushes nearby, where the thick branches kept the rain at bay. A deep breath filled my chest as I watched The Wrangler help the bipeds up from the ground. I couldn't hear what he said to them, but before I knew it, he was escorting them away.

I wondered how they ended up in the middle of the grass just outside the woods.

CATHERINE

Sheri brought us both mugs of steaming hot tea and sat across from us in one of the plastic chairs in the employee lounge. Gloria and I were huddled on the one soft piece of furniture in the building: a dilapidated tweed loveseat with a weird stain on one cushion. I took that one and let Gloria have the unstained one, but, honestly, it was out of reflex because I was still far too freaked out to make conscious decisions right now.

"Do I need to send security into The Haunted Wood?" Sheri asked for the fourth or fifth time.

"Uh...no," my voice still shook, "I'm sure we were just imagining things."

"Well, if security has any Ghostbusters on their payroll, I'd say now is the time," Gloria offered. I elbowed her to keep quiet.

I didn't want to make a big deal out of this. It wouldn't help us investigate. It had to be part of the effort to terrorize Charlotte or the Forests—or us, right? Maybe Kenny Davenport was behind this too?

Sheri sighed. "I'm gonna go call Tom Carson. See if he's in yet. If not, the night ops manager should be on duty."

She walked away, and I cast Gloria a glare. "Why did you tell her we saw a ghost?"

Gloria rolled her eyes. "Because we did?! C'mon, Cat, that was *not* normal. And it looked real. REAL!" Her hands trembled as she reached out to grab my arm. "Did you hear what she said?"

"Yes. Something like, 'Where is he?' and then, 'You're next.'"

"She said, 'You're next' more than once!" Gloria shook her head, her eyes still wide with terror.

"Well, we need to figure out what we're going to tell Mr. Carson because his daughter is getting married in," I looked at my watch, "two days now, and there are a lot of weird things afoot."

"You can say that again!" Gloria agreed. "It was Harriet Mackie, wasn't it?"

I sighed. "She was wearing a wedding gown...so it appears that way."

"Why wasn't she at St. Michael's like she was supposed to be?" Gloria looked frazzled, and she never looked frazzled. She also had a streak of mud on her left cheekbone. "I don't know if I can ever go back in The Haunted Wood again."

I sucked in a deep breath and let it out with a *whoosh.* "Come on...buck up, Buttercup—this is probably a big ploy to get us to stop investigating whoever is trying to intimidate Charlotte."

"But they're trying to intimidate *us!*" Gloria snapped. "Why? What did we do? Why would they be targeting us?"

Sheri walked back in carrying a cordless landline phone. "Mr. Carson is on the phone. He's calling from home. I think the night manager woke him up."

My voice quivered as I answered, "Hello?"

"Ms. Lyon? It's Tom Carson."

"Hi, Mr. Carson. Sorry to wake you up—"

"No, no. I told my people to call me if there were any issues. Charlotte was there tonight checking on things for the wedding. She said she saw something too…"

"A ghost?" I asked, my voice barely audible.

"She said it was a strange light, and there were some weird noises, and then it started pouring rain."

"How long ago was she there?"

"An hour ago? I'm not sure. She just got here, so I was actually still awake. She's pretty upset. She's in the living room with her mom right now. The wedding is only two days away, and we're all scared something bad is going to happen. Have you gotten any further in figuring out who might try to ruin my daughter's wedding?" The concerned father's voice lingered in my ears as I scrambled to think of how to answer him.

"Well, I'm assuming what we saw in the graveyard tonight in The Haunted Wood is all part of the scheme. It's escalating, and we're still trying to figure things out. I'm going to speak with Kenny, the best man, before we leave work in the morning. We also found a book about poisons, along with poisonous plants in big urns on either side of the altar. I don't know for sure if Charlotte planned for those to be there, or if someone else ordered them, but they're making some of the animals in the park sick. Once we found the book nearby, it seemed like maybe it was done deliberately—"

"A book about poisons?" He sounded incredulous.

"I know…it seems like maybe it's not related, but so far everything has related to Harriet Mackie, the bride who died at St. Michael's in 1804. She was poisoned shortly before her wedding. We believe the ghost we saw tonight was someone pretending to be her." It was someone pretending, right? It had to be…but it looked so real…

I swallowed hard as the realization set in. We had to take this seriously. It seemed like a practical joke, but Charlotte's life could actually be in danger. "Make sure your daughter is extra careful about anything she drinks. I—I still think there's a good chance someone is just having some fun at her expense, but we don't know if they really wish her harm. This seems to be escalating."

"I understand." Her father let out a deep sigh. "I remember hearing that ghost story when I was a kid, but I never thought—"

"It seems like someone is using that story to harass her. I'm glad you told us she was in the park tonight. Now—who knew she was going to be here? That's the real question."

Mr. Carson was silent for a moment. "I'll have to ask her. I mean, I'm sure Walker knew, possibly Kenny since he works in the park. Jocelyn probably knew, and Marci, her wedding coordinator. Could be her other bridesmaids knew."

I made a mental list of everyone he'd named. They were our suspects. "Anyone else you can think of?"

"Her mother and I, of course." There was a brief pause. "Ms. Lyon?"

"Yes?"

"Can you come to the rehearsal dinner on Friday night? I'll talk to Jim and make sure it's okay, but I'd like to have you and your friend Ms. Bress there. Maybe you can help us prevent anything bad happening. And then, of course, I hope you know we'd love to have you both at the wedding and reception on Saturday."

"Thank you, Mr. Carson. We'll be working both of those nights anyway, so we'll be in the park."

"My wife and I really appreciate your help. Jim and Janelle do as well."

"We're happy to help, sir." I nodded to Gloria, and she smiled.

"You said you're going to talk to Kenny when he gets in?" Mr. Carson asked.

"Yes, sir."

"If you get any inkling he's behind this, I want you to call me immediately. I'll be in the office by seven a.m." His tone changed from worried to authoritative. I hoped for Kenny's sake he wasn't involved.

"Yes, sir, I will."

I hung up the phone and relayed his side of the conversation to Gloria.

"Okay, sounds like our next step is Mr. Davenport's office, then we need to get to the library at College of Charleston to find out who checked out that book. In the meantime—we need to dig into Marci and Jocelyn a little more deeply. I haven't eliminated them as suspects."

I squeezed her hand. "Feeling better then?"

She took a deep breath. "When your hand's in the lion's mouth, you always have to ease it out."

ZOE

It had been a while since we'd visited the River Cats, who were aptly named since they lived near the small river that wound its way through one side of the park. The castle where I met Cat and Gloria overlooked the river, and there was a boat ride that moved along a track that used part of the river for its course as well.

"Delta? You there?" I called out. The River Cats mostly communicated through body language, and they seemed able to tune out other forms of communication, but I saw her tortie head pop up from behind a rock.

She made her way over to me, scampering agilely across the rocks with her two closest pals, Brooke and Beck. "Zoe, hey! How are things?"

I waited for the trio to arrive before answering, "Everything good here? No more issues with Scar and his thugs?"

"All is well," Delta confirmed, and her two companions nodded.

"We have a bit of an issue," I shared. "Our senior clowder member, Mr. Cool Cat, is missing. Haven't seen him in a long while, and we're a little worried about him."

Delta tapped one paw on the ground as she tilted her head, the night breeze ruffling her whiskers until she shook her ears. "He didn't age out, did he?"

"Age out?" I had not heard this term before, and didn't expect the River Cats to know something I didn't. They kept to themselves, and I'd only become friendly with them when I learned Scar was giving them a hard time, wanting to take over their territory.

"When one of us gets old, The Wrangler comes for them," she explained solemnly. Brooke and Beck looked at the ground.

"I don't think it's his time yet." I refused to believe it—was I being naïve? He seemed healthy, just a little slower, the last time I'd seen him. He was still eating well. Sleeping a lot—but that was all of us, really. Cats loved their sleep.

"I see. Which one is he? What does he look like?"

"Medium-sized tom, short hair, light silvery tabby markings," I explained. "Usually grumbling about how things just aren't the way they used to be."

Delta turned to Beck and Brooke as if to check in with them before shaking her head. "Haven't seen him."

"You haven't had anyone get sick from eating the mice around the park, have you?" I checked. "One of our members, Sass, was taken out of the park to get treatment after eating a sick mouse."

"We mostly eat fish," she reminded me. As if to flaunt their fishing prowess, she studied the water for a moment. It swirled and glistened under the moonbeams shining down on it. In a heartbeat, her paw shot out, dipped under the current, and she pulled it up with a small silvery fish speared on her claws.

Incredible. "Wow, I'm always impressed when you do that."

She licked her lips. "Happy to teach you sometime, if you'd like."

"We've got bigger fish to fry at the moment, but maybe I'll take you up on that someday." I'd heard that phrase in a biped television show. I was pretty sure I'd used it correctly.

She just cocked her head and stared at me as if to ask, "Fish to fry? What's that mean?"

I dipped my head in farewell and raced back toward our home base. There were a few more clowders to check in with, and I planned to visit them all tonight.

CATHERINE

It had been a long night, but we were finally ready to talk to Kenneth Davenport, the head of landscaping.

There was a huge complex beyond the public areas of the park that was invisible to guests thanks to fencing and landscaping. Traveling in a golf cart, we were able to cross behind the Goldilocks ride and the Jack & the Beanstalk attraction to access the landscaping offices.

Enormous buildings that resembled airplane hangars housed the parade floats, special seasonal displays, workshops where set pieces were built and repaired, and the costuming shop where employees' uniforms and character outfits were designed and created. It was the backstage hub of Fairytale Forest, and there were as many behind-the-scenes employees who worked in this section of the park as there were ones who interfaced with customers every day.

Park custodians rarely came out this way, though if we had bigger equipment—vacuums, trash compactors and other items—that required repairs, we sometimes needed to make the trip. I hadn't been out here since dropping off a broken floor cleaner a few years ago. This area had their own team of custodians to keep everything neat and tidy.

On one side of the landscaping building was a sprawling greenhouse where seasonal plants were grown from seed, and tons of outdoor equipment such as lawn mowers, weed eaters, pruners, and the like were stored in small sheds across from the greenhouse. In between the building and the sheds were mountains of mulch, stacks of straw bales, and piles of gravel.

We made our way to the office at the spot where the greenhouse met the rest of the building. That was where we'd find Kenneth Davenport.

Kenny was a young man in his late twenties with spiky auburn hair and a thick matching beard. He bore a hulking figure, like a lumberjack with broad shoulders and arms and legs the size of tree trunks. He was intimidating until you heard him laugh, which he did often—including now, as we approached. The deep sound rumbled through the entire building as we made our way toward his office through rows of poinsettias being grown for the winter holidays.

I knocked on the metal door frame. "Mr. Davenport? Can we talk to you for a minute? We were sent by Mr. Forest." Dropping the owner's name was usually an effective way to get any staff member's attention.

A frown flickered across his face as he hung up his phone, but it was quickly erased by a smile. "Come in, come in." He gestured with both of his arms, waving us inside.

His office was sparsely decorated with one shelf that contained a dozen or so thick binders. I expected a land-scaper to have plants in his office, but there were none. There was also one photograph with him and a young woman, whom I assumed to be his girlfriend, Ellie. The cement-block walls were painted a strange shade of mint-green.

"What can I do for you two ladies? It's not very often anyone from the front office comes to visit me out here in the sticks." He chuckled and cracked his knuckles. The sound seemed to echo off the bare, utilitarian walls.

"Well, we're helping out with Charlotte Carson's upcoming wedding," I explained. "We've been noticing a few strange things around the park, and we wondered if you knew about any of them."

"What kind of strange things?" His thick auburn brows arched in surprise, but I didn't know him well enough to ascertain if it was genuine. With everything Marci said about him, I was disinclined to believe anything he said. He was a jokester, a prankster, she said. Maybe interrogating him wasn't worth our time.

"Well, the latest is there are two big urns of poisonous berries near the altar where Charlotte and Walker will be getting married, and we found this book nearby." I held up the library book titled *Toxic Plants of North America.* "And, well, you're the head of landscaping, so if anyone would know about the poisonous berries, it would be you. Some mice and rats ate them, and then the cats that ate them got sick—"

"I'm well aware of the importance of the critters in the park," he said, the smile vanishing from his bearded face. "I would never plant anything toxic that could harm them."

"Well, how do you explain this then?" I pulled out my phone and showed him the photo I'd taken of the berries. It wasn't the best quality since it was dark, but with the flash on, you could sort of see them.

He took the phone from me, studying the screen. "That can't be..." He scrubbed his hand down his face. "Those urns are supposed to be full of *Callicarpa.* I'm not one hundred percent sure, but these look like…" He pulled out his own phone, scrolled a few screens, then pointed it at the photo on my phone. "It's a plant identifier app."

His eyes widened as the results loaded. "No! That can't be right!"

"What is it?" Gloria asked. I noticed she had scooted to the edge of her seat.

"*Atropa belladonna*," Kenny revealed, sounding more serious than before. "It's deadly nightshade. Truly poisonous. I would *never* plant that. The urns are supposed to contain *Callicarpa*—beautyberry. Hold on." He typed something into his phone and tilted the screen toward us to reveal a lovely plant with clusters of plum-colored berries.

"That's beautyberry?" Gloria's eyebrow rose as she questioned him.

"Yes, ma'am. Here, I'll show you the order." He turned to his computer, navigated with his mouse, inputted a few words and then turned the screen to show us a huge spreadsheet.

I blinked a few times. "What are we looking at?"

"These are the lists of plants ordered for fall planting—back in the spring. We plan about six months ahead." He highlighted a row. "Four *Callicarpa* plants, see?"

"Is this the actual order form or just the spreadsheet with the orders?" I questioned.

"It's just the spreadsheet of what we planned to buy, but I give this to my admin assistant, and she finds the best prices and puts the orders in."

"And who is that?" I asked.

"Well, it's usually my full-time secretary, Alice Simmons. But in the spring we had an intern from the College of Charleston. I—" He squinted and pursed his lips for a moment. "I'd have to check with Alice, as the intern's name isn't coming to me at the moment."

"What did you say the name of the plant that's actually there is called?"

"It's *Atropa belladonna*, also known as deadly nightshade." He turned away from his computer and fully faced us now. "I know Walker and I have the reputation of playing practical jokes, but I wouldn't mess around with poisonous plants. I promise."

"Did you have anything to do with a chess piece showing up near the altar?" I asked next. "One with an owl and the number twenty-two on the bottom?"

He tossed his head back with laughter. "Well, I did have something to do with that. It was actually my girlfriend's idea. She just wanted to mess with Walker a bit. You know, she used to date him."

"Yes, we heard something about that," I said. "Was your girlfriend actually here in the park?"

"No, ma'am, she is up at Clemson in grad school. She'll be here for the wedding though. She gets in tomorrow afternoon."

"Is that her in the photo?" I pointed to the frame on his shelf next to the binders. The young woman in question was a blonde with high cheekbones and cat-shaped eyes heavily rimmed in black liner.

"Yes, ma'am. Isn't she a beaut? She's studying horticulture. When she gets her master's degree, she hopes to find a job down here in the Charleston area. Maybe at one of the plantations—they all have extensive gardens, you know. We're both from this area. Her parents have lots of connections."

"Gotcha. So, she studies plants, but you're sure she didn't have anything to do with poisonous berry plants showing up in The Haunted Wood?" I confirmed. No matter what he said, she was still a viable suspect—even if she was away at school. She might have been angry that Walker had moved on and was marrying Charlotte. It wouldn't be that hard for her to drive down to Charleston. Clemson was about four hours away.

"No, of course not." Kenny was adamant. "She wouldn't want to hurt the kitties here either. And, yes, she knows about them."

"When was the last time she was in Charleston?" I followed up.

He looked at the large calendar spread across his desk. "She went to Charlotte and Walker's co-ed shower with me in September. I've been up to Clemson once since then. After the wedding, I won't see her until Thanksgiving Break."

He was owning up to the chess piece. Maybe I could get him to admit to some of the other shenanigans. "Do you know anything about a bouquet of dead roses that was delivered to the Forests' beach house a week or so ago?"

He blinked a few times. "Dead roses? Why would someone send dead roses?"

From the surprise etched on his features, I believed him.

"So you still have no idea how the belladonna plants got there," I questioned again.

"No, ma'am, but I'm glad you've pointed them out. I'm going to go out there this morning and make sure they get removed. If I can't get my hands on the beautyberry plants by Saturday, I'll just add some pretty purple mums." He shook his head. "I knew I should have checked to make sure everything looked right. We've just been busy planning the transition from fall to holidays. Does the arch look okay? Nothing wrong with it?"

"It seems fine to me," I said, though I didn't pay nearly as much attention to that as I did the berry plant. And, truly, all of it was a little hazy after running for my life from what sure looked like a ghost. "Will your girlfriend be at the rehearsal dinner Friday night?" I checked. I wanted to speak with her in person.

"Yes, she will. Ellie is my date for the wedding as well." He smiled and laced his fingers together.

"Okay...one more question, then we'll get out of your hair." I smiled and reached into my fanny pack to pull out the silver locket. "Have you ever seen this necklace before, or the painting inside?"

He took the necklace from me and looked at it closely. I'd handed it to him with the locket popped open, so he could easily see the tiny painting inside. He scrutinized it for a moment, and I watched his face closely to see if any signs of recognition appeared, but they didn't.

"What does this have to do with the price of tea in China?" he grumbled, looking up at us. He dropped the locket into my outstretched hand like it was a hot potato.

"We found it in the park, and we thought it might have been a reference to the bride," I explained.

"The bride? You mean Charlotte?" His eyes narrowed as he tried to make sense of it. "Oh, it was a painting of a bride?"

"Yeah," I answered, "a dead one."

His face went pale.

ZOE

For some reason, I kept finding myself drawn to the woods area where all the activity had been. The fact that all those bipeds had been in and out of the gates all hours of the night when we were prowling around made me feel like it must be related to Cool's disappearance. There was a cat clowder that lived near the woods, but they were even more insulated and reclusive than the River Cats. They were rarely, if ever, seen. As a matter of fact, I often forgot about their existence.

But there was a chance they had seen our missing tom, and I couldn't leave any stone unturned. That was another biped expression I learned from watching TV.

As I grew closer to where I believed their lair was, behind a huge tree and concealed in a dip between the tree and the fence that enclosed the woods, the fur on my back rose. I was being watched—perhaps by one of the members of this elusive clowder, perhaps by one of Scar's thugs. I was probably too stubborn in my insistence that I make this inquiry alone. But I was certain my presence would put the Woods Cats on edge—adding others would only exacerbate the problem.

"Hello?" I called into the night. Shadows of the tree branches danced in the moonlight as I crept closer to their den.

My paw landed on a dry twig and made a loud cracking sound as my weight fell on it. My tail shook as a scent enveloped me. "Hello? I come in peace," I added this time.

Then, four pairs of glowing green eyes surrounded me. My hackles were not only raised; they were shooting skyward. I froze in place, waiting for one of these creatures to speak.

"Please, I don't mean any harm. I am looking for my lost friend," I announced, making my voice as smooth and steady as I could despite the panic coursing through me.

Was it Scar? Vinny?

"Step into the moonlight," came a deep, rumbling voice that almost sounded like a purr.

Without hesitation, I moved forward into a swath of light that created a silver streak on my gray fur. I sat up, my tail curling around me as I tried to force my fur back down to my skin. I blinked as the light flooded my vision, no doubt turning my pupils into thin slits.

Then the four pairs of eyes materialized as four sleek

black toms as they stepped in perfect sync into the light, one on each side of me. I gasped as I took in their menacing presence. One yawned, showing sharp white teeth.

"I-I'm looking for an older light gray tabby tom," I stammered. Then I took a deep breath and straightened my spine. I was Zoe, Leader of the Courtyard Clowder, and I refused to be intimidated by these four large toms.

I looked from face to face as their features gradually relaxed. They all seemed to be checking in with each other, mumbling in some sort of insider code I couldn't understand.

"Hello? Have you seen him? His name is Mr. Cool Cat, Cool for short," I added.

The male facing me head-on stepped a bit closer, staring me straight in the eyes. "Yes, actually, a tom by that description was taken by a female biped a while back."

"What?! Are you sure?" My heart, which had just calmed down from the scare they gave me, kicked up into a racing beat again.

The tom to my left yawned. "Yes, she stuffed him into a basket and carried him away. They came from beyond the gates, where all the commotion has been of late."

"Do you know what she looked like? Do you have a description?" I knew it wasn't Cat or Gloria—so who else could it be? The Wrangler was a male.

"No, sorry, didn't get a good look, just saw the biped was wearing a…what do they call it? The long gown with no legs? Only the females wear those, correct?"

"A dress?" I questioned.

"Yes, a long white dress that dragged on the ground."

"Okay, thank you." I nodded in gratitude to all four of them. "I appreciate your help. If you see her or him again, would you let me know? My clowder and I live—"

"We know where you live," said the tom to my right.

"Oh, okay. I'm Zoe," I introduced myself.

"We know," they said in unison.

"And you four are—?"

"Never you mind our names. We're known as the Night Ninjas. That's all the information I can disclose," came the voice from behind me.

I whipped around to see the fourth tom, but…they were all gone.

Fourteen

"After this wedding, I'm planning to sleep for like a week," I told Gloria as I whipped my Rogue into a parking space in the tiny visitors' lot near the library on the College of Charleston campus.

"We're going to need Mr. Forest to give us another week at the beach house," Gloria sighed as she unfastened her seat belt and opened her door.

"Seriously. I have been thinking a lot about what you said—that trying to prevent a murder is way more stressful than trying to solve one. You are one hundred percent correct." I looked up at the massive building with *Marlene & Nathan Addlestone Library* in big letters on the façade.

"Well, why would I lie? Though I am still not completely convinced Charlotte's life is at stake. I feel like someone just wants to ruin her special day." Gloria shuddered. "That ghost, though. That was a bit over the top, don't you think?"

"I hope you're right that it's just someone trying to get under her skin, but I'm not taking any chances." Before we headed inside the large modern-looking library, which looked a little out of place among the historic buildings on the College of Charleston campus, I pulled the book about poisons of North America out. "While you were in the bathroom this morning, I read the entry on *Atropa belladonna* in the book. You've gotta check this out." I handed the small blue book to her.

She adjusted her reading glasses and read aloud, "*Atropa belladonna*, also referred to as 'deadly nightshade,' was commonly considered to be the Devil's property, and anyone who ate the berries was punished for eating the Devil's fruit. The plant was a symbol of danger and betrayal in art and literature, and *Atropa* is derived from Atropos, one of the Three Fates in Greek mythology, who could snip a person's string of life and bring about their death. Belladonna means 'beautiful woman.' In the Renaissance era, women used the plant to enhance their looks because it dilated their pupils."

She looked at me with a wary smirk. "It does sound like something a jealous woman might use to poison her competition. Would Ellie, Kenny's girlfriend, do such a thing? She used to date Walker—do you think he broke up with her to date Charlotte?"

"We should ask Marci or Jocelyn," I suggested. "You did catch that Ellie is studying horticulture, right?"

"Oh, I did not miss that fact," Gloria assured me. "But what of Kenny's claim that Ellie hasn't been here since September?"

"Well, maybe we will get lucky, and the person who checked this book out is our suspect." I held it up when she returned it to me. "Though I don't know why Ellie would check out a book from this library if she goes to Clemson. Wouldn't she use their library?"

"She might have checked out the book here over the summer?" Gloria theorized.

"It's possible. Hopefully we can find out whose account this book is checked out on." I marched toward the entrance with Gloria in tow. She was looking perky in polka-dot pants and a vibrant turquoise shirt, whereas I looked like I'd worked every bit of eight hours last night. And I'd dropped ketchup on my peach-colored shirt. Sigh.

We walked inside the enormous stone building, noticing how empty it was. "I guess students aren't beating down the library's doors at eight in the morning, huh?"

Gloria laughed. "I don't suppose so. Where do we go to ask about the book?"

I pointed to a sign. "Over here." We walked up to a desk where a bored-looking young woman sat. She wore a fuzzy bubble-gum-pink sweater and had fuchsia hair. She obviously loved the color.

"Hi, good morning," I greeted her in my friendly, non-threatening middle-aged lady voice. "We found this book over at Fairytale Forest, and it appears to have come from this library." I laid the blue *Poisonous Plants of North America* book on the desk.

"Oh, are you returning it?" She raised one dark brown eyebrow, arching it above layers of sparkly pink eye shadow.

"Well, we were hoping you could tell us who has it checked out," I explained. "You see, it's very important that we talk with the person who left it in the park."

"Fairytale Forest—what is that, exactly?" She wore a silver nose ring in one of her flared nostrils.

She clearly wasn't from around here. By her accent, I'd say she was from the Midwest. Probably Ohio or Indiana or something. "It's an amusement park just minutes from here."

"Oh," was all she said, taking the book off the desk. She scanned it with a black plastic wand with a red light and set it on a metal cart to her left.

"Wait—we need it back!" *Oops, that was a little bit louder than what's acceptable in a library.* "Especially if you're not going to tell us who checked it out!"

"Is there a problem out here?" A short, wiry white man appeared from an office behind the information desk. His thin lips were outlined by a neatly trimmed goatee, and his beady brown eyes were obscured behind plastic-framed glasses with thick lenses.

"Simon, these ladies are asking to know who had this book checked out." She pointed to the blue book on the cart, next to a taller one covered in the same type of material, only it was green.

He scoffed, picked it up, scanned the title, and lifted his chin to address us. "I'm sorry, but we cannot reveal the name of the patron who checked out the book. We take patron privacy very seriously here at Addlestone Library. Thank you for your understanding in this matter."

"I do understand," I argued, "but the person who left this book in the park is wanted for questioning by the police."

Gloria shot me the stink-eye.

Well, they *would* be wanted for questioning, if the police were involved. But I knew Mr. Forest wanted to keep the police out of things as much as possible.

"If the police have a need for information, they are welcome to try to get it. There are laws protecting patron privacy," the goateed man continued. "Patron privacy is a cornerstone of library science, ma'am. You can have the name of the patron who checked out this book over my dead body." He puffed out his chest and indignantly scoffed again.

I sighed. "Alright, well, can we have it back then?"

"Absolutely out of the question," he said in a snooty tone. He glanced down at the computer monitor on the desk and frowned. "The patron who checked it out owes a substantial fine. It is several months overdue."

A lightbulb went off in my head. Several months? Perhaps

Gloria's theory about Ellie checking out the book over the summer was plausible.

"Well, thanks anyway." I rolled my eyes as I ushered Gloria away from the desk. I'd taken a photo of the book, the title page, and the page with the entry on *Atropa belladonna*.

We walked back out into the sunshine—the temperature had probably climbed ten degrees just since we'd been inside. I made my way down the sidewalk until Gloria tapped my arm. I stopped walking. "What?"

"You took that pretty well—being told no." Gloria smiled.

"Oh, I have another plan."

She laughed. "Ah, I see. And are you going to fill me in on this plan?"

"I'm going to text Jayden to see if he knows anyone who works at the library." I pulled out my phone and scrolled my contacts to find Jayden Forest. We'd exchanged numbers after he left his summer job at the park his parents owned. He and his girlfriend, Nora, helped us solve the last murder. Now he was a student at College of Charleston, and I was sure he had connections. He was a Forest, after all.

WE GRABBED BREAKFAST AT A CUTE LITTLE CAFÉ NEAR CAMPUS while we waited for Jayden to text us back. "He's a college student, so who knows how long it will take." I cut a piece of French toast and popped it into my mouth. *Mmm...butter and cinnamon.*

Gloria seemed to be enjoying her omelet. "He lives on campus, right?"

"I think so, why? You have a better idea?"

"We could stop by the Forests' house on King Street. I

mean, we're kind of in the neighborhood. Maybe they know how to get ahold of him faster?"

I pointed my fork at her before taking another bite. "Brilliant as usual." I chewed and swallowed. "As soon as I wreck this French toast, we'll head over."

Next thing I knew, we were navigating the narrow streets of the historic district till we arrived at the Forests' beautiful multi-million-dollar home. There was the stone owl perched in the doorway as I remembered from my previous visit here. Truth be told, I was pretty sure Gloria just wanted to see their house for herself, since she hadn't been with me the other time I was here.

I expected an employee to answer the door but was actually shocked to see it was Jocelyn Forest Whitaker herself, and she was positively glowing. I hadn't actually met her before, so I prepared myself for an awkward introduction.

But Gloria knew her and saved me the trouble. "Well, Mrs. Whitaker, it's positively delightful to see you! How are you doing, honeybun? It's been just about forever."

Jocelyn nearly shrieked, she was so happy to see Gloria. She threw her arms around my friend so emphatically, it nearly knocked Gloria over. "What are you doing here? It's been way too long!"

"Sweet girl, we are looking for your brother," Gloria said.

"Which one?" Jocelyn's brunette eyebrow rose as she ushered us inside. "Well, don't stand here in the foyer, ladies. C'mon in. Can I get you something to drink? Coffee? Sweet tea? Moira, can you get these lovely ladies some refreshments?" she called into the kitchen.

"Sweet tea would be divine," Gloria said. "Do you know Catherine Lyon? What'll you have, Cat?"

"Sweet tea would be great, thanks." I extended my hand. "It's nice to meet you, Jocelyn."

"Oh, Catherine Lyon!" Jocelyn's hands flew to her face

like the kid in *Home Alone*. "I can't believe I'm finally getting to meet you in person! My parents talk about you nonstop!"

My cheeks flushed as she ushered us into a formal parlor. "Well, I hope they say good things."

"The very best things! I know what you've done for my parents and the park, and I couldn't begin to express my gratitude." She looked at me in awe. I believe younger generations might say she was "fangirling" me, which I would have never expected from anyone in a million years, and it felt downright weird. But also cool.

"It's my pleasure," was the only response I could think of.

"Now, which of my brothers are you looking for and why?" She folded her hands together in her lap as Moira arrived with a tray of macarons and three glasses of sweet tea.

I took a sip of my tea before answering, "Jayden. We worked with him this summer, and he's such a great kid. We're having an issue and need some information at the college library, and we thought he might be able to help us."

She excitedly clapped her hands together. "This wouldn't be in reference to Charlotte's wedding, now would it?"

Gloria and I exchanged glances. "Well…perhaps," I admitted.

"Daddy said he put you on the case. I know a lot of weird stuff has been popping up."

"Do you know if Charlotte has received any threats personally? Anything to her home or work?" I assumed Mr. Forest or Mr. Carson would let us know if she had—so far everything had been either directed at us or the park. Why? If Charlotte was the intended victim?

"No, ma'am, not that I'm aware of. I'm sure she'd tell me. I'm the matron of honor, you know." She beamed proudly, then patted her lower abdomen. "Just hope I won't have any issues fitting into my dress. The Bean has had a bit of a growth spurt in the past two weeks."

"Congratulations!" Gloria cooed. "I just know you're going to make the most amazing mama. What a lucky little boy or girl."

Jocelyn grinned. "We're so excited! Thank you." She took a bite of a pink macaron, then dabbed at her lips with a napkin. "Now, back to Jayden. I can give you his phone number, but I know he's in class all morning. He has a break around noon for lunch."

"I texted him, but I wasn't sure what his schedule was like," I revealed. "Maybe he'll get back to us soon. But, actually, since we're here, I do have a few questions for you because we're trying to figure out who is harassing Charlotte and whether or not they pose an actual threat to the wedding."

"Sure, of course." She nodded eagerly. "I'm happy to help in any way I can."

"You obviously know Charlotte very well," I began. "We've been getting to know her, as well as the other members of the wedding party and the wedding coordinator."

"Oh, yes. Marci." Jocelyn rolled her eyes. "You met her?"

"Yes…do you have concerns about her?"

"No, no, not concerns." Jocelyn waved her hand to brush away that notion. "She's just…well, she's clingy, you know? Charlotte's tried to ditch her for years now, and she just keeps coming back. She's harmless, of course. Those dresses she wears. She's a bit much, you know? She never grew out being a theater geek."

I smiled. "She does seem to like frills and lace."

"Yeah, I think she's going for a retro vibe, but…she ends up looking like a pastel cupcake, you know?" She sighed. "I shouldn't be catty like that, I'm sorry. She's a perfectly lovely woman. She's just…"

I let her off the hook as far as finding an appropriate descriptor for Marci was concerned. "What do you know about Kenny Davenport, the best man?"

"Oh, he and Walker go back a long way, all the way to childhood. Kenny is a smart man, but he's an immature goofball at times," she said, echoing what we'd heard about him from others.

"Do you think Kenny would harass Charlotte and Walker with some pranks before the wedding?"

"Oh, yeah, absolutely—" She nodded emphatically. "Kenny and Walker live for pranking each other."

I went down my mental suspect list. "What about his girlfriend, Ellie?"

Jocelyn's face darkened a bit. "Well…I don't know her that well, to be honest. I've only met her a few times. And I know she used to date Walker."

"Do you have any idea if she would try to interfere with the wedding? Does she seem vindictive?" I saw no reason to beat around the proverbial bush about this—or even the actual deadly nightshade one.

"Well, like I said, I don't know her that well. I mean, it's possible she and Kenny could be teaming up for some of this stuff. You said you talked to Kenny?"

I didn't say that…but okay.

"We did talk to him, earlier this morning," I shared. "We found some poisonous plants in the park near where the wedding is supposed to take place. They killed some mice in the park, and a cat who ate one of the mice."

"Oh no!" Jocelyn's hand flew to her mouth. "Not one of the cats!" Her eyes began to tear up. "Which one?"

"I'm not sure," I answered. "It made another sick—also from eating an affected mouse."

"Kenny knows better than to put any plants like that in the park," she cried. Moira was there in a heartbeat with a box of tissues. "Sorry, I'm…well…the pregnancy has made me very emotional. And I…I've always been attached to the cats. Daddy used to get so mad at me for trying to play with them when I was little."

Interesting. I wondered if she knew Zoe or any of the other cats in her clowder.

"Anyway, you said you needed to talk to Jayden?" She dabbed at her eyes again with the tissue.

At that exact moment, my phone buzzed with a text from him.

"Oh, here he is now!" I skimmed the message, a smile coming to my face. "He said he's between classes but has time to grab lunch if we're near campus. I think I might take him up on that offer."

Jocelyn smiled too. "Good. Is there anything else I can do for you?"

I shook my head. "I can't think of anything, but thank you for your insights. If anything strange happens, will you let me know? Otherwise, we'll see you at the rehearsal on Friday. Your dad asked us to poke around and be on alert for anything fishy."

The lovely young woman stood up and ran her fingers through her wavy brunette locks. "I'm looking forward to seeing you both again, and I am sure everything will go off without a hitch."

"I sure hope you're right," Gloria said, and she gave Jocelyn a hug before we made our way back out to my Rogue so we could head back to campus.

We declined to tell her about the ghost.

Fifteen

Jayden recommended a little sandwich shop that was within walking distance of his next class. We grabbed a booth and waited, and sure enough, here he came along with Nora. I was surprised to see her, but I guessed that meant they were still an item. She had really come out of her shell since meeting Jayden when they worked together this summer on night shift custodial at Fairytale Forest. I liked to think Gloria and I had a hand in bringing the two of them together.

We not only solved mysteries, but we were matchmakers too! Nice work if you can get it.

"Hey!" he greeted me when I stood up, and next thing I knew, he was flinging his arms around me for a bear hug that popped my vertebrae.

"Wow, you just did better than my chiropractor!" I teased him.

He laughed, and then Nora gave me a hug while Jayden gave Gloria, who was much more petite than me, a gentler hug. "What's up, ladies? I hear you're coming to the wedding this weekend?"

Nora beamed. "Oh, yay! Normal people I can hang out with! I have a feeling there will be a lot of rich, uppity folks."

Gloria and I both chuckled. It was pretty funny that an eighteen-year-old thought we were better company than her boyfriend's family friends.

"Your dad has asked us to be on the lookout after a few strange things popped up that might be related to the wedding. We sure miss you guys being in the parks—you could have helped us investigate."

"Yeah, Dad filled me in—something about a bouquet with a weird note that showed up at the beach house, a locket with a painting of a dead bride, and some chess piece that seemed to be a reference to our house on King Street," he went through the list of clues—for lack of a better term. "Do you think the person leaving all this stuff is trying to intimidate my family or Charlotte or both?"

"Well, there've been a few new developments." I looked at Gloria, and she nodded, but she looked uneasy about telling Jayden.

Before I could share, a waitress who looked about Jayden and Nora's age came over to take our orders. I felt like we'd just eaten—that French toast was still sitting in my stomach, so I just ordered a small salad, and Gloria did the same. Jayden and Nora both got burgers and fries. *Ah, to be young again and eat whatever you like!*

When she walked away, Jayden's dark eyes pierced into mine. "What happened, Cat? You look a little spooked by it."

"Um, 'spooked' is an apt word," Gloria agreed, crossing her arms over her chest.

"Look, I haven't told your dad all of this yet, and it's going to sound pretty crazy, so…bear with me. I hope you don't try to have us committed after this."

"What is it, Cat?" Now Nora looked concerned as well.

"Okay, well, first of all, the reason we texted you. We found some plants in big urns on either side of the altar where the wedding ceremony is supposed to be held—they're poisonous berries. Some of the mice on the property ate them and died, then a couple cats ate the mice and got sick—one passed away, sadly."

Nora gasped. "Not Zoe though, right? Please say it wasn't Zoe!"

I shook my head. "Not Zoe, but one of her group's cats got sick, and another is missing."

"That's not good. How did poisonous plants get into the park? I can't imagine the gardeners would plant something like that. They know better!" Jayden insisted.

"I know…and we talked to Kenny Davenport, who is the head gardener and also the best man, and he denied ordering those plants. He said what he ordered was a different species that isn't toxic. Anyway—Zoe found a book near the altar. A book of North American poisonous plants."

Jayden's mouth gaped open. "That's what you texted me about, right? A library book?"

"Right. It was stamped with Addlestone Library—College of Charleston. So, we went to the library this morning to find out who checked it out, figuring that would be a big clue to who left the book there and probably put the poisonous bushes in those urns too."

"And?"

"Well, that's why I texted you. They wouldn't tell us. We got a big spiel about patron privacy and all that. But we hoped you knew someone who worked there because we really need to know," I explained.

He exchanged a worried glance with Nora. "Do you still have the book?"

I shook my head. "No, they confiscated it from us." I bit my lower lip.

Nora looked at Jayden and smiled. "Well, I just so happen to work at the library—a few hours a week. I work in a different department, but I can access the circulation database. I would need the exact title to look up in the catalog."

"*Poisonous Plants of North America*," I told her. "It was published in the 1920s. Small, faded blue book. I can text you some pictures."

"Wow, a hundred years old," she gasped. "I can probably find out on Friday night. That's when I work next."

"Oh, you won't be at the rehearsal dinner?" Jayden asked. "I thought you were able to come with me."

"Sorry, Jay. I will be at the wedding though." She shrugged.

I nodded, my jaw set with resolve. "If you can find out, please let us know."

"So is that it?" Jayden's gaze bounced between the two of us. "Or is there something else?"

I watched Gloria's chest move up and down as she sucked in a deep breath in anticipation of me telling Jayden and Nora what we saw in The Haunted Wood last night. We had fared pretty well as far as moving on from the scare of our lives was concerned…but the prospect of sharing our experience with someone else made chills dance up and down my spine all over again.

"So…you're probably gonna think we're absolutely nuts, and I'm sure there's a completely reasonable explanation for what we saw, but let me just preface the following little tidbit with this: *it looked real*. You might even say it looked legit. Do y'all say 'legit' still?"

Nora and Jayden exchanged glances, and Nora giggled. "Go on," Jayden pleaded, already at the edge of his seat, leaning forward with anticipation.

"Well…no easy way to say this, but here goes: last night when we went to check out the berry bushes…" I looked at Gloria, hoping she wasn't going to pass out when I relayed the details. "We saw what looked like a ghost. In the fake graveyard."

"What?!" Jayden burst out laughing, and Nora clutched his arm, her brows knitting together.

"I know it sounds funny, but—a ghost isn't part of the wedding ceremony, right?" I asked. "Like they weren't testing something for the wedding last night, were they? Do you know anything about there being a ghost? Like a projection of some sort? But it didn't look like a projection…and it spoke."

They both stared at me, wide-eyed and blinking slowly.

I was bungling this, wasn't I? I shook my head. The image was indelibly burned into my brain. "Guys, it looked real. I'm not joking. It was a ghost bride. And she was wailing and looking for someone. She said 'Where is he?' and then she said 'You're next! You're next!' Just like the note attached to the bouquet of dead roses we got at the beach house."

Nora huffed out a breath. "That sounds absolutely terrifying. Maybe I won't go to this wedding after all."

Jayden erupted in laughter again. "Oh, come on, guys, I'm sure there's a perfectly reasonable explanation for this. It's probably the same person who planted the locket, right? Don't people say a dead bride ghost haunts the graveyard at St. Michael's?"

"That's what we've heard," I nodded, "but how did she get from St. Michael's to Fairytale Forest? Can she swim?"

Gloria and Nora both gave nervous chuckles at that question.

"So, we're pretty sure this is someone in Charlotte's circle who is trying to sabotage her wedding, and it has to be someone who has access to the park." Jayden steepled his hands on the table as if in deep thought. I'd seen his father wear a matching expression.

Before I could say anything else, our food arrived, and we began to dig in. Jayden started throwing out ideas for suspects. "I assume you talked to Kenny, the best man? He's known for being a prankster, but this is pretty elaborate... even for him."

"Yes, we spoke with him this morning, and he swears he ordered a different berry bush for the wedding ceremony spot. He said he would never knowingly plant something poisonous where the mice and cats had access to it. And, well, I don't think he could pull off a wedding gown, no offense."

"Well, Charlotte used to work at the park when she was younger—pretty sure my dad said she worked in the Witches Cauldron Candy store. Can you figure out if anyone she worked with is still there? Maybe they have it out for her?" Jayden suggested.

"That's a good idea," Gloria said, "and we're looking into Kenny's girlfriend. Apparently she used to date the groom."

"Oh?" Jayden's brow rose. "But how would she access the park?"

"I'm assuming she could access it through Kenny," I said. "And get this—she's getting a master's degree in horticulture from Clemson. We just can't figure out why she would check out a book from the College of Charleston library, unless it was checked out in the summer when she was home. Which reminds me, we still need to know who had it checked out. The librarian said there's a fine on the account for the book because it was overdue."

"So this might all hinge on an overdue library book?" Nora asked, her face looking more animated than I'd ever seen it before. "This is quite the story—dead bride ghosts, poisonous berries, silver lockets, chess pieces, threatening notes on bouquets. It's pretty crazy!"

"And we can't even tell if there's an actual threat." I heaved a weary sigh. "And if there is an actual threat, is it to Charlotte or to the park in general?"

"And," Jayden took my question a little further, "does it have anything to do with the other two bodies found in the parks?"

I was still trying to figure that out myself.

It was almost like someone was trying to mess with all of us.

ZOE

Seeing Sass sashaying around the courtyard like her normal self filled me with hope. If she returned to the park alive and well, maybe Mr. Cool Cat would too.

But I had to do something I didn't want to do.

I needed to go talk to Scar and his thugs to see if one of them saw someone leaving the park with Mr. Cool Cat. Not that they would tell me, but surely if a blonde female biped in a white gown was leaving with a cat, they would notice. Their clowder was based near the entrance to the park. They had the best vantage point to see bipeds coming and going.

I gathered up Moony and Snow and told them the plan.

"You want to do what?" my brother questioned.

"I don't think it's a good idea to go over there," Snow warned.

"And why do you say that?" I remembered what Amber said about seeing Snow cavorting with Vinny.

"Because they're mouse turds?" His whiskers twitched.

"Truer words were never meowed, but I can't shake the feeling Cool is out there somewhere, and until I know what happened to him, I won't be able to stop worrying about him. Don't you think I have enough to worry about without wondering where that old tom got off to?"

Moony looked at Snow and tilted his head. "She has a point."

"If I can't get my two most reliable toms to help me, then I will go ask Amber and Ziti. I'm sure they'd do just as good of a job protecting me as you two would—if not better."

"Well, now, wait a second," Moony said, his tail swishing back and forth in annoyance.

Ah, yes, appeal to their egos—that was a solid plan, wasn't it?

"C'mon," Snow said, "let's go."

Feeling a good deal of self-righteous smugness, I followed the two toms up the main street of the park. No one was around but some security bipeds and a few cleaning bipeds. They were used to seeing us scampering about and sometimes even helped us by pointing out vermin—especially near the restaurants where they were trying to steal a meal. I understood why the bipeds liked helping us—if we took care of the rodents, they didn't have to. Just another example of bipeds using quadrupeds to do their dirty work.

Their *delicious* dirty work. I licked my lips.

We reached the end of the street and veered off to the thick cluster of bushes that surrounded a three-story stone building just to the right of the park gates.

"Psst, Vinny?" I called out. "You around?"

The three of us sat there, waiting for the tuxedo cat to appear. Sure enough, his mostly black body with its white vest and facial markings appeared from behind a dumpster. He looked right at home by a dumpster.

"Whaddya want?" he snarled as he approached.

"Yeah, he's in a great mood tonight," Moony said. "This oughta be fun."

"I just want to ask you a couple questions." I kept my voice as light and pleasant as I could, what with their vile scent filling the air. Or was that the dumpster?

Vinny slinked into the light, followed by two of his thugs, Alfie and Frank.

"First of all, we were very sorry to hear about Klaus." I sat up straight, my tail curling around me. "Please accept our sincerest condolences."

"That's a rather civil thing to say, thank you," he acknowledged with a nod. "But I know you're really after info, so what is it?"

I didn't mind cutting to the chase. The sooner we got out of here, the better. "I know you said you haven't seen Mr. Cool Cat, but did you see a blonde biped female in a white dress carrying a basket any time in the not-too-distant past? Leaving the park?"

His gaze bounced from one comrade to the other before landing on me again. "So what if we did?"

"We think she might have taken Cool." My tone did not betray my frustration. I was one cool kittycat.

"Well, if she did, there's not much we can do about it." One shoulder rose ever so slightly. "Bipeds gonna do what bipeds gonna do."

"Did you recognize her? Does she work here?" I persisted.

"Dunno," he said. "And even if I did, not sure I would give the info to you."

"So you may or may not have seen a biped female matching that description, and she may or may not be an employee of the park," I confirmed.

"That summarizes it quite nicely," he sneered.

"I pray you don't need any information from us in the

future." I tapped a paw on the ground. "Because you're outta luck if you do."

"Hey," Moony's gaze shifted toward me, "don't you have some valuable information about the poison making mice and cats sick around the park—you know, what made Sass sick and what killed Klaus?"

I turned to my brother, immensely proud of him for coming up with that little brilliant nugget. "Well, yes, I suppose I do, but I don't think Vinny and his crew are interested in hearing it."

One of his thugs headbutted him, leaving Vinny scrambling to explain, "Well, I don't think the biped female in the white dress with the basket works here, but I believe she is friends with someone who does."

I jumped on that. "What makes you say that?"

Vinny shared, "She was with him the times I've seen her."

He's seen her multiple times?

"And who is he? Where does he work?" I prodded.

"I'm not sure. He doesn't usually come in and out the main employee entrance, only when he's been with her." He looked smug, like he was well aware he'd given me *just* enough information to be unhelpful.

I blew out a breath that made my whiskers flutter, echoing my frustration. "Fine. Don't eat any berries in the woods, or any mice that are acting weird or sick. The berries are poisonous."

"Gotcha. Well, thanks for the info." He gave the feline version of a cocky grin.

Some blonde female biped in a white dress, carrying a basket, had taken Mr. Cool Cat, and I intended to find out who she was and what she'd done with him.

Sixteen

CATHERINE

"Bingo." I pointed to the computer screen next to the time clock. The very first thing I did when I came into the facility services building was look to see when Charlotte Carson worked in The Witches' Cauldron candy store. Then I cross-referenced that time period with other employees who worked in the candy store that summer.

"Well?" Gloria's eyebrows arched toward the colorful wrap around her hair.

"Guess who worked in the candy store the same summer as Charlotte?"

"Tell me!" She bit her lip in apparent anticipation.

"None other than Walker Buckley, Ellie Ferguson, Brittany Dawson, and Ruth Buckley." I smacked the monitor in my excitement. "And Jocelyn Forest, of course."

"The groom, his ex-girlfriend, and all of Charlotte's bridesmaids!" Gloria smiled. "Nice work. They go back pretty far, and that means they're all familiar with the park."

"It doesn't narrow down our suspect list, but now that we know, we can ask some pertinent questions." I rubbed my hands together. "Tonight is the night. We'll get to meet everyone at the rehearsal." Before I could say anything else, a yawn took over my body, stretching my mouth wide.

"Did you get any sleep at all?" Gloria asked as we took turns clocking in.

"Hardly a wink. I don't know how I'm gonna make it through the night. But I'm going to have to buck up. This wedding hinges on us. No pressure, of course."

"I tossed and turned all afternoon," my coworker confessed. "Plus, my baby girl called and woke me up to say she's coming for Thanksgiving." She looked me up and down. "You brought something else to change into, right?"

"Oh, that's good news about your daughter. Yeah, I brought something nicer to wear for the rehearsal, but I don't think we're gonna get much work done before that anyway. We're meeting with Mr. Forest at five, right before the rehearsal starts at six, and before that, I want to go scope out the…area." I sucked in a deep breath.

"You mean where we saw the ghost?" Gloria whispered.

I flashed her a wary look, my gaze darting around to make sure none of our coworkers, or worse, yet, our boss, was listening in. Sheri wasn't very happy about the lack of actual work we'd done this week, but we couldn't help it if her boss's boss's boss had given us different orders.

Us not getting a few toilets cleaned was better than the entire park shutting down because something terrible happened again, right?

"Come on," she grabbed my hand, "let's get out there while it's still light."

"What time are they shutting down the park?" They sent out an email, but I read it when I was half-asleep, so I didn't remember. The hours, days, weeks—they were all starting to run together at this point. I glanced at my watch, but time seemed almost meaningless to me right now.

"Four o'clock." She checked her own watch. "I'm sure they're ushering everyone out now, so we'll be going against the traffic, but that's okay. We can take the back way, behind the tree."

She was right—most visitors completed one side of the park, visited the tree, and then did the other side. Not very many people took the winding path that ran from the back of the courtyard to The Haunted Wood. We were going to take advantage of that.

The wind had kicked up, and the layers of clouds obscuring the sun gave me pause. "I sure hope it doesn't rain tonight. Do they have a backup plan for the rehearsal or for the wedding ceremony if it's raining?"

Gloria shrugged. "That's a good question for Mr. Forest when we see him."

I nodded in agreement. "Well, come on. I'm sure we won't see anything in the daylight, but we can check for more clues. See if anything seems out of place before it fills up with people."

I thought I heard Sheri calling my name as the door to the facility services building shut with a thud. She'd just have to wait until we were done with this assignment. We couldn't serve two masters, after all.

The Haunted Wood gates were unlocked, and the place looked completely normal and non-scary in the daylight. The trees were still full of leaves and decorated with lovely Spanish moss. The archway now bloomed with fresh flowers in fall colors, intertwined with twigs, pinecones, and berry vines. The decorators had made it look less dead and spooky and more beautiful, wedding-appropriate. And the two urns on either side of the altar were filled with a different type of plant. The black poisonous *Atropa belladonna* berries were gone.

It just looked to be a normal fall day. They'd done an incredible job making the gravestones look like old, weathered stone markers. But they were clearly made out of something lightweight—fiberglass was my guess.

I froze as my gaze zeroed in on one gravestone. I didn't remember seeing it before.

Gloria stopped beside me, her eyes catching on the same stone I was staring at. A whimper caught in her throat as we both stared in disbelief.

"That wasn't there before, was it?" her voice shook.

"No…" I stepped closer to it, running my fingers over the top. I studied the "engraving" again just to make sure I wasn't seeing things.

Charlotte Carson
May 15, 1997 - October 15, 2022

"That date is tomorrow. Her wedding day. Take a picture," she said, her voice barely more than a whisper. "We have to show this to Mr. Forest and Mr. Carson."

As I got my phone out of my fanny pack to snap the photo, she silently grabbed my arm, dragging my attention to where her eyes focused on a different gravestone farther back. I gasped when my gaze raced over the text.

Catherine Lyon
February 27, 1969 – October 15, 2022

ZOE

I crept out of the bushes, warily watching the feet of all the bipeds ambling past. Turning to Hank, who was curled up in a big ball of orange fluff, I cleared my throat to try to rouse him. When he didn't budge, I tapped him on the side with my paw.

"Hank? You okay, buddy?"

He mumbled something incomprehensible.

"Why is everyone heading toward the exit? It's too early for closing, right?" I jiggled him a little with my paw.

I was asking Hank because he seemed to have a better sense of time than anyone else in the clowder. He was extra sensitive to anything that deviated from the normal routine.

"They're shutting down the park early for some event," he answered, not even bothering to open his eyes.

"Oh, how do you know that?"

"That's the word on the street," he explained. "Storybook Street."

He was referencing the main street through the park, where most of the shops and restaurants were. He liked to go hang out behind the seafood restaurant right at park close when they threw out any leftover food. He and a couple other older cats from nearby clowders usually got first dibs —even though the employees at the restaurants knew they weren't supposed to feed us. Some of them just couldn't resist. And, of course, Hank and Company weren't about to pass up that golden opportunity.

I huffed, "I have to find Cat."

"Suit yourself." He yawned, stretching his jaws wide enough to show all of his teeth. Then he was asleep again a heartbeat later.

I knew I should go by myself. After all, I didn't want to attract any attention from the departing bipeds. I could travel through the bushes to a certain point, but then I'd have to cross over an area without cover. It would help if I knew where Cat might be, or was it too early for her to come in? I wasn't sure. It was almost always completely dark when I saw her.

I started to pick my way through the bushes when Snow blocked my path. I was about to yell at him to get out of my way when I noticed something rather disturbing…

Vinny was beside him, and the snarls on their faces told me they had no intention of letting me pass.

CATHERINE

We were supposed to meet Mr. Forest in his office at the top of the tree in the middle of the park. My stomach lurched as we hopped on the elevator to carry us to the top floor. That gravestone had my name on it. It had my correct birthdate—how did they get that?—and my death date listed for tomorrow.

I knew Charlotte was a target, but…why? Why was someone targeting ME?

My legs felt like jelly as we hit the carpeted hallway, rushing toward his office and not even bothering to check in with the administrative assistant.

"Wait, you can't go—"

We didn't heed her warning, walking directly into Mr. Forest's office, where he was in the middle of giving a toast. Several people I recognized were gathered around him: his wife, Janelle; Mr. Carson and who I assumed to be Mrs. Carson; plus Charlotte and who I assumed to be her groom and the other members of the wedding party.

177

"Oh, Ms. Lyon, Ms. Bress! You're a little early, but please join me in a toast. Janelle, do you mind?" He gestured toward his wife, who immediately sprang into action to ensure we had champagne.

Gloria and I exchanged a look that was a cross between "We aren't dressed for this" and "Should we do the toast or tell him what we just saw first?"

We both smiled to the best of our abilities as Janelle handed us each a flute of champagne. She turned to her husband with a beaming grin. "Go ahead, honey."

"As I was saying," Mr. Forest chuckled in his jovial way, "we are gathered here this weekend to celebrate the union of two much-loved young people, ones I've known since you were both knee high to a grasshopper." He lowered his hand to indicate their small stature as kids as everyone joined in the laughter. "Why, it seems like just yesterday you weren't big enough to ride the Gingerbread Man coaster, and now you're getting married in the park we all hold dear. Janelle and I hope that, tomorrow, as you say 'I do,' it will be the first promise of many you will make to each other during a long and happy life together."

He raised his glass, and we all echoed "hear, hear" and sipped our champagne.

As soon as everyone began to break into smaller groups to converse, I approached Mr. Forest, who was standing with his wife and the parents of the bride. "I'm sorry to interrupt, and I know our meeting isn't for another forty-five minutes, but something has happened that we need to urgently discuss with you."

He simply nodded and smiled at his guests before announcing, "I must step away for a few minutes to take care of some business. We'll return shortly. Come, Tom. Follow me, ladies." He gestured toward the bookcase behind his desk.

He pulled out a book, and like something out of a movie, the bookcases parted, sliding along a hidden track behind them and revealing a dark, open space. "I'll get the light," Mr. Forest said as he stepped through the passageway. "Don't be afraid. It's my safe room."

If I wasn't already freaked out by seeing ghosts and grave markers with my name and birth-death dates on them, then this was a one-way ticket to Panic Town. My heart felt like it was going to give out as I stepped between the bookcases into the dark, waiting for Mr. Forest to turn on the lights.

When he did, a cozy, windowless room illuminated before us. There was a gas fireplace, which came on with the lights, two love seats perpendicular to each other, and two leather wingback chairs that looked perfect for reading classic literature and smoking a pipe. Not that I would ever do the latter, but, wow, did it give that vibe. Everything was dark wood and deep shades of green with black, brass and cranberry-red accents like an Irish pub.

"What is this place?" I looked around in awe. Gloria, standing beside me, seemed too stunned to speak.

"I didn't even know this was here!" Tom Carson whispered.

"No need to whisper. This place is soundproofed. Have a seat and tell me what's going on, ladies." He gestured to the seating, and Gloria and I both plopped down on one of the loveseats beside each other without further thought.

I laced my fingers together in my lap like I was about to pray. I felt like prayer might be a good follow-up activity to this conversation, so it seemed apropos.

"Catherine?" Mr. Forest prompted me again.

I swallowed hard, and Gloria put her hand on my thigh for reassurance. "We've been…investigating, and a couple of concerning things have popped up. We went to see if there was anything unusual in The Haunted Wood area where the ceremony is slated to be, and we found…um…some poisonous plants had been placed in urns on either side of the altar. Nearby was a book about poisonous plants of North America. We were chased off by a ghost—a woman in a bridal gown—and it started pouring rain, and then we went to talk to Kenny in landscaping, and—"

"Wait, back up," Mr. Carson interjected. "You saw *what* in The Haunted Wood? Did you say a ghost?"

"Uh…yeah…" I nodded, noticing how dry my throat suddenly was. I wasn't sure if that was the effect of the champagne or just my nerves about telling the boss of the park and the father of the bride the chilling things we'd witnessed in the last twenty-four hours.

Mr. Forest and Mr. Carson exchanged looks that seemed to be a cross between "These ladies might be wackos" and "What the heck are we going to do to keep Charlotte and the park safe from a ghost?"

"I don't know if it was real," I stammered, "I mean—it looked real. She said, 'Where is he?' And then, 'You're next! You're next!'" I even tried to imitate the ghost's creepy high-pitched voice. "Well, we were pretty scared—as you might imagine—and we hightailed it out of there, but it started raining cats and dogs, and we fell somewhere outside the gates in the mud. Next thing I knew, we were heading to talk to Kenny. I really don't remember much between seeing the ghost and talking to him."

Mr. Forest steepled his hands just like his son had done earlier today. "Did you tell him what you saw?"

"No," Gloria answered for me. "We were scared as all get out! Talking about it only made it seem like it really happened, and, at that point, it seemed better to pretend it didn't. We needed to find out how those poisonous bushes got there because cats were starting to get sick from eating the mice that had eaten them, and we even lost a cat—"

"I heard about that." Mr. Forest frowned, bowing his head. "I know Kenny wouldn't have—"

"No, he denied putting them there. He said he didn't know how they got there. He claimed he ordered a different plant with berries back in the summer, so he wasn't sure how the order got changed."

Mr. Carson huffed out a long sigh. "Did you tell him about the other stuff?"

I nodded. "The only thing he'd cop to was the chess piece. He said he didn't have anything to do with the book, the bouquet, the locket or the poisonous berry plants."

"I see." Mr. Forest scratched his chin.

"But that's not everything," I said. "After we left his office, we clocked out and went to the College of Charleston library to see if we could find out who checked out the book of poisons we found in The Haunted Wood because it was stamped with Addlestone Library."

"And?" Mr. Forest's brow rose.

"No luck. The librarian said it was a violation of patron privacy to disclose who had checked the book out—"

"But someone's life could be in danger!" Mr. Carson protested. "My daughter's life! That's more important than who checked out a blasted book!"

"The poisonous plant was *Atropa belladonna,*" I disclosed. "Deadly nightshade. It was in the book. Whoever left the book must have also changed the order—so it has to be someone who had access to Kenny's ordering system. I don't know anything about it, so—"

"His girlfriend," Mr. Carson immediately accused. "His girlfriend, Ellen Ferguson. She used to date Walker. She interned here this summer in landscaping and worked at the candy shop one summer when she was in college. She would have had access to everything in his office." He turned to Mr. Forest. "I knew letting her work with Kenny was a bad idea."

Mr. Forest scrubbed his hands down his face. "So, we think it's Ellie. Doesn't she study horticulture? Why would she need a library book from a college she doesn't even go to anymore?"

"I don't know, but is that her?" I pointed to the entrance to the safe room. "With Kenny? The blonde?"

Mr. Carson nodded. "Yes, Kenny said she arrived yesterday."

I clutched Gloria's arm. "The ghost was blonde…"

"But that's not all," Gloria said. "Cat, the gravestones…"

I was confused now. Because if it was truly Ellie—how did she know me? Did she send the bouquet to Mr. Forest's beach house? Did she leave the locket so I would find it? I couldn't quite make sense of those things. Why would she try to mess with *me*?

"What gravestones?" Mr. Forest and Mr. Carson asked in unison, their deep voices hanging in the air as I tried to unscramble all my words and thoughts.

"We went today, just before coming here, to check things out. The berry plants have been replaced. But…but there was a new development."

"Something with the gravestones?" Mr. Carson asked.

"Yes, I'm assuming the scene shop made the gravestones, but there are two new ones today. One is for me—and one is for Charlotte. They have our death dates listed as…tomorrow…"

ZOE

"What's the problem? Why won't you let me pass?" I glared at Snow and Vinny, who united like a big fur wall in front of me. I dodged to the left; they dodged and blocked me. I shifted to the right; they shifted as well.

"You need to do something for us," Vinny said.

"Why are you with him?" I directed my hiss at Snow. "You're betraying me?"

Snow's head fell back, and he beat his paw against the ground as if he found my outrage the funniest joke he'd ever heard. "Oh, Zoe, you really are naïve, aren't you?"

"You helped me defeat Scar and his thugs when your biped died," I reminded him. "Why help me if you're going to turn around and help the enemy we just defeated?"

"Well, 'defeated' is a strong word, Z," Vinny answered for him. "You see, you may have humiliated us, but it was far from defeat. All it did was make us more determined to punish you for your actions."

"Punish me?" I scoffed.

"Yes, you've been cavorting with the bipeds, and it's time you come clean. You need to be deported from the park immediately, and if you won't willingly turn yourself in to The Wrangler, then we'll force you to."

I scoffed again. "Oh, really? First off, what's in it for you, Snow?"

"It became immediately apparent that my power was limited with your clowder," he answered. "You'd never give up your leadership role, and you have instilled a great deal of power in your brother and those shameless hussies constantly vying for his attention, Ziti and Amber."

"Not Amber. It's Ziti and Princess who are vying for his attention, ya meat ax," I hissed. "You've spent all this time with us, and you don't even know us? No wonder you didn't care that Mr. Cool was missing. Heck, you probably have something to do with his disappearance."

"Well, no matter, because you guys are all losers. I'm now third-in-command, right behind Vinny, and I've been promised leadership of your clowder when we take it over—as soon as you're deported from the park."

I stood my ground. "Oh, please. That is not happening. How do you think you're going to manage that?"

"Well, if you don't turn yourself in to The Wrangler by the time of the biped celebration tomorrow—we're going to ruin the entire thing for the bipeds and make it look like your fault. If their party gets ruined, and they blame you, your precious biped friend won't want anything to do with you. She'll be the first to ask The Wrangler to round you up!" Vinny threatened.

"Oh, yeah? We'll see about that." I stamped my paw on the ground. "Go ahead and try."

Snow leaned in and hissed in my ear, "It'll be my pleasure...."

Eighteen

Before we rejoined the crowd waiting in the main part of the office, I asked Mr. Forest, "Are you going to call the police? Maybe they should come out and interrogate Ellie? Have her arrested before she can wreak havoc with the wedding?"

"Not until we have more evidence," came his response. "When are you supposed to find out about the library book? You said Jayden and Nora are helping with that, and she works at the library tonight?"

It seemed like everything was hinging on this book. "Yes, where is Jayden? He's not here yet?"

"No, he had a late class, but he'll be here in time for the rehearsal dinner. Hopefully he can let us know then. Now you all go on back out there and have some more champagne. I'll rejoin everyone shortly, after I make a call to send some security officers out to the Wood. I'm going to have them remove those gravestones and examine them for clues."

Gloria pulled me aside as soon as the sliding bookshelves closed behind us. "Well, what are we going to do now? Should we look for evidence that she changed the plant order or created the gravestones?"

"I don't know." My gaze roamed over to the young woman for a moment before settling again on my colleague. I had a novel idea. "Why don't we try simply talking to her first?"

"Lead the way," Gloria said as I scanned the room to see if our target had moved.

Ellie Ferguson was sitting with Jocelyn, Charlotte, and their three corresponding men in the window area that overlooked the back side of the park. The sun was starting to sink faster now that it was nearly five o'clock. The idea was for the rehearsal to start at the same time the wedding would begin—just before dusk. So soon, the bride and groom's entourage would need to make their way to The Haunted Wood.

We didn't have a lot of time, and I wasn't sure how to isolate Ellie—but she wasn't in the wedding party, so maybe she would stay behind to talk to us instead of going with the others. How could I make her stay?

She was into horticulture, right?

What kind of knowledge did I have of horticulture?

Well, I knew a little about the various poisonous plants of North America, particularly one *Atropa belladonna*, after having access to that book. I could also figure out a way to see if Ellie knew the story of Harriet Mackie.

I glanced at Gloria, trying to send her the subliminal message that I might need help tying all this together, and she shot me back a look that said, "I got you, friend." I was lucky to have such a steadfast, loyal partner, wasn't I?

Before I could crash their conversation—which appeared

to be about wine—a familiar voice filled the office area with its overly perky soprano. "Hey, everyone! Sorry I'm late, but I need the bridal party to follow me. We need to get in place for rehearsal now. The officiant is ready to meet you all and give you some instructions."

Marci. She was wearing a voluminous pumpkin-colored frock with ivory suede boots I feared would get ruined in the mud after the torrential downpour we had last night. Her blonde locks were pinned up in a complicated updo, and she carried a brown leather portfolio with a South Carolina Society stamp on it in gold.

The group's murmuring slowed down, and everyone but Ellie and a man I recognized as Jocelyn's husband from the photos on Mr. Forest's bookcase followed Marci out the door. Before he left, Kenny pressed a kiss to his girlfriend's cheek.

Jocelyn's husband nodded politely at Ellie before traversing the room to join his father-in-law and the bride's father in conversation, leaving the young woman standing awkwardly by the window. I got my first look at her. She didn't look like a vindictive jilted lover hellbent on ruining her ex-boyfriend's wedding to another woman. She was really quite an average, plain-looking young woman in her mid-twenties, with a long waterfall of golden-blonde locks, a small upturned nose, and icy blue eyes. She wore a dusty pink lace dress with tall brown Western-style boots.

Those looked better equipped for the mud.

If she had been out in The Haunted Wood the last two days pretending to be a ghost and "planting" (ha, she was studying to be a horticulturist, get it?) fake gravestones to harass Charlotte and myself, she knew darn well the ground was saturated by the recent rains. Perhaps she dressed with that in mind?

We didn't just march over there like two assassins homed in on their mark. No, we flitted like the social butterflies we were pretending to be, all cool and casual-like. She must know who we were, or at least who I was, if she made a gravestone for me. If she completed an internship here in the park over the summer, she would have been here when we solved the first murder case.

"Hi," I offered her a warm, friendly smile, "you look familiar. Have we met before?"

Her cheeks flushed pink as her eyes darted around the room as though looking for someone to save her from two scary middle-aged women. Oh, yes, she looked nervous. Probably because she knew we were the two celebrated sleuths who had kept Fairytale Forest from facing a ruined reputation in the wake of two bodies being found on the premises.

"I don't think so." She straightened up tall, but she was still shorter than me and around the same height as Gloria.

"Oh, hmmm," I extended my hand, "well, it's a pleasure to meet you, then. I'm Catherine Lyon, and this is my colleague, Gloria Bress." I grasped her hand, feeling how cold and clammy her skin was against mine. After I gave it a firm shake, Gloria offered her own.

"Nice to meet you." She seemed distracted, looking at the door and not making eye contact with us. The stance of guilt.

"Mr. Forest said you worked here this summer as an intern," I began. "That must have been a fun gig. Was it a stepping stone to a career?"

She bit her lip and sucked in a breath, seeming to be deciding on how she wanted to answer my question. "Yes, it was helpful to gain some experience in the field before beginning my master's degree in horticulture at Clemson."

That checked out.

"Oh, horticulture—does that mean you got to work under your boyfriend's tutelage?" I probed a little deeper.

She gave me a look that proved she was having a hard time taking me seriously. I didn't care. I would press onward.

"If you're talking about Kenny, then yes," she said. I noticed she didn't have a Southern accent.

"You're not from the South, are you?" I questioned.

She shook her head. "No, I'm from Ohio. I did my undergrad at College of Charleston and fell in love with the area… and, well, other…" She trailed off without answering.

Was she talking about Walker?

How could I ask that without seeming like a total creeper?

Gloria elbowed me stealthily. "We were just at the college today, actually, lovely campus."

"Oh? Why would you go there?" She tapped her foot twice and stared at Gloria.

"We were checking out the library," Gloria answered. "We recently found a book left behind here in the park, and it was stamped Addlestone Library, so we decided to return it."

"The library is nice," Ellie said. "Spent a lot of time there as an undergrad. What was the book?"

Gloria glanced at me, a signal for me to take over. "It was called *Poisonous Plants of North America*," I explained, then studied her facial expression. It didn't change at all—not an eyebrow arch, a facial twitch, an eye narrowing or widening…nothing. Either she really wasn't intrigued by my statement at all, or she was one heck of an actress. "We've been finding a lot of interesting things around the park, now that I think about it."

"Yes," Gloria continued, "like a silver locket with a copy of an old painting in it. It was a little worrisome considering the subject of the painting and what we're gathered for here this weekend."

"Worrisome?" Ellie repeated. "How so?"

Gloria deferred to me again, so I explained, "It was a painting of Harriet Mackie."

I left it at that and searched her face for signs of recognition.

She shrugged. "Sorry, I don't know who that is."

Oh, she was good. Very good.

"She was a bride who died just before her wedding ceremony that was to be held at St. Michael's church in the historic part of Charleston. They say her ghost still haunts the graveyard."

"Oh," she said dismissively, "I'm not into ghost stories much."

"Hey, I just remembered something I saw in that poisonous plants book," I changed the subject. "You're studying horticulture, so maybe you would know about it?"

"What's that?" Now we got the slightest eyebrow arch.

"Do you know anything about *Atropa belladonna?*"

"Oh, deadly nightshade?" she fired back without a thought. "Sure, it's a poisonous plant. Makes sense it was in your book."

"Not my book," I clarified. "A book from Addlestone Library at the College of Charleston."

"Right. Sorry, you said that." She smiled. "Well, I could talk about plants all night, but I think they're getting ready to head out to The Haunted Wood for the rehearsal."

"Good idea," I agreed. "Have you seen it yet? They've done a great job with it."

"Oh, yeah. It looks great." Ellie nodded and smiled. "I love the archway with all the flowers. Kenny and I actually picked them out and ordered them when I was working for him."

This time, it was my elbow sharply stabbing into Gloria's side. Ellie joined the other group, Mr. and Mrs. Forest, Mr. and Mrs. Carson, and Jocelyn's husband, and kept ourselves several paces behind them so we could take a different elevator.

Once we had the privacy of our own elevator car, Gloria rubbed her side. "You poked me a heck of a lot harder than I poked you."

I patted her arm. "Oops, sorry, friend. Um…how did we do? Did we learn anything?"

"Well, she just admitted to ordering the plants for the wedding this summer. I think it's totally possible she ordered the belladonna. We'd just have to get into the ordering system and see."

"Right. I think we can get someone to help us. Who's the administrative assistant out there? Let's give her a call while we're walking to the rehearsal," I suggested.

Gloria rubbed her hands together. "Let's do!"

ZOE

As soon as Snow and Vinny were gone, I took off for my clowder. Everyone was starting to rouse from their naps, and in the midst of their groggy yawning and stretching, I had a chance to process everything I'd just learned.

First of all, Snow had betrayed me. Amber was right—he was cozying up to Vinny, and all that sweet-talking he did to me was only because he was trying to move up in our ranks. Well, sorry, buddy, but I would never demote my tried-and-true hunters for some schmuck who spent his formative years as a house cat.

Secondly, Scar had come up with an ingenious idea to get rid of me: force me to give myself up so I didn't bring harm to my biped friends.

They were threatening to ruin the BHD—big hairy deal—event that was happening in the park tomorrow evening. I didn't know how exactly, but they were going to pin it on me if I didn't out myself to The Wrangler.

Which I didn't even know how to do.

I needed to talk to my clan, my clowder, before making any rash decisions. Oh, how I wished Mr. Cool Cat was here to advise me. His wisdom was much-needed right now.

"What's up, Sis? You seem on edge." Moony slid up, brushing his tail against me before walking away, then circling me again. "Did something happen?"

"Yeah, you could say that. Gather everyone. We need to have a team meeting."

"Team meeting?" His whiskers scrunched up.

"Biped saying, sorry." I looked around at the crew, and it seemed everyone was accounted for except Mr. Cool Cat and Snow, of course.

Ziti and Amber moved into position right in front of me. Moony and Ice sat next to them. Hank was in the center, in his usual loaf form. Daisy, Sass, and Princess were in the rear, all three looking somewhat attentive—shocker!

"Okay, all, there's been a new development," I announced. Murmurs started to burble and gurgle among my feline fam, but I held a paw up to quell the rumblings. "Just listen, please, then you'll have a chance to weigh in. First thing: Snow has defected. He sold us out to Scar and Vinny, and they want me to turn myself in for fraternizing with the bipeds."

"What does 'fraternizing' mean?" Ice asked.

"It means being friendly with," I explained. "They're jealous I've become so close to Cat and Gloria, and they know Cat and Gloria have also helped us out. They've threatened to ruin the wedding happening here tomorrow if I don't get myself picked up by The Wrangler beforehand."

There were shouts of, "They can't do that!" and "How dare Snow betray us like that!"

Then Sass asked, "Wait, what's this wedding you speak of?"

"A biped is getting married tomorrow in the woods," I explained. "I know, I was like, what does that mean, and, basically, it means two bipeds pledge their undying love to each other and to put up with each other for the rest of their lives."

"Ewww!" all the cats in my clowder spat in unison.

"Yeah, exactly, but they are really into it. It's a big celebration with music, dancing, and food. That last one could be good for us, but let's concentrate on the issue at hand. If I go, Scar, Vinny and Snow are gonna make a move to take this clowder over. And I know you might all find me annoying, but surely you'd rather have me than Scar as your leader."

"Yes, of course!" came a shout from my brother.

"We love you, Zoe!" came from Ziti and Amber.

The others didn't shout out enthusiastically, but they did look rather worried about what a Scar-led Regime might be like.

The mice are not any tastier on the other side of the fence, you know?

"So we have to figure out a way to keep Scar and his thugs from ruining the wedding and blaming us."

"How do they even know it's happening?" Hank voiced. "I didn't know about it, and I know everything that happens around here thanks to my…ahem…connections."

"Well, you didn't know Snow was cavorting with the enemy, did you?" I didn't mean for it to come out so snarky, but it was definitely snarky. I wished my clowder had been paying more attention, then maybe we wouldn't be in this mess. But maybe it was my fault. I'd been so focused on helping Cat and Gloria, and also on finding Mr. Cool Cat, maybe I was blind to what was happening with Snow right under my very own whiskers.

"Sorry, Zoe," came Hank's apology.

"It's okay. We just need to work together. I'm sure Snow has given them all the intel he's gathered in the time he's been with us. It's up to us now to outsmart them. I have some ideas. Gather around; we need to make sure there are no spies, and no one overhears us…"

Nineteen

CATHERINE

By the time we arrived at The Haunted Wood, Marci seemed to have things well under control. She stood at the end of the aisle, telling each bridesmaid when to go. The family members and friends who were not part of the wedding party all sat in the metal chairs on either side of the aisle. The male members of the wedding party stood on the right side of the altar while the officiant, a bearded middle-aged white man wearing a gray suit, stood in the center. On the altar, someone had placed three white candles, two tall taper ones, and one thick pillar candle in an ornate antique brass holder.

There were two other bridesmaids who hadn't been present in the penthouse office. I nudged Gloria, "Are they Ruth and Brittany?"

"No clue. Let's go sit by Mrs. Forest. She'll tell us."

"Good plan!" I smiled at her, then led the way to where Mr. and Mrs. Forest sat in the second row on the bride's side.

"Who are the other bridesmaids, and where did Ellie go?"

I whispered, suddenly noticing Ellie wasn't sitting on the groom's side.

"The other bridesmaids are Ruth and Brittany, friends of Charlotte's from college. Ruth is also Walter's sister. I'm not sure where Ellie went, but she interned in the park this summer, so she knows her way around. She might have gone to check out the rehearsal dinner with Walker's mom."

"Where is the rehearsal dinner going to be?"

"It's at the Magical Mushroom," she said. "Walker's parents made all the arrangements with the chef—it's customary for the groom's family to take care of the rehearsal dinner. I think Ellie was helping Mrs. Buckley with everything as well since she knows the park. She and Kenny are probably going to be engaged soon, you know. We might be having another Fairytale Forest wedding before too long."

I heard a loud throat clearing and turned to see Marci scowling at us. Our conversation had apparently gotten too loud. *Oops!*

I turned to Gloria and whispered, "I want to go keep an eye on Ellie. Can you stay here and make sure nothing happens?"

"I don't know what I'm going to do about it," she replied. "But there are plenty of strapping young security folks here to help." She looked over her shoulder at the half circle of security guards standing to the side.

"Oh, good. I'm glad they're here." I glanced around to see if I could spot Jayden. "I really wish they'd get us the info on the library book."

"Maybe they haven't been able to track down the person who checked out the book either," Gloria said with a shrug.

"Maybe. But I have to believe they'll come through. It's not exactly a smoking gun, but it's at least a smoldering poisonous berry."

She laughed as I stood up. Marci stopped Charlotte and

her father from proceeding down the aisle, shooting me a glare. "Is there a problem, Ms. Lyon?"

"Oh, no, don't mind me. I'm just going to the restroom. Carry on!" I grinned as I headed up the left side of the rows of chairs and toward the gate. I had a few other tasks in mind that would hopefully solidify the identity of our suspect.

I TOOK ONE OF THE GOLF CARTS THAT HAD BEEN LEFT BY THE gate and trucked on over to the backstage area where the landscaping office was. I knew Kenny was with the wedding party at the rehearsal, so I was hoping to poke around without anyone in the office.

I parked outside the greenhouse, thankful I still had the master key card Mr. Forest had given me so I could access any areas of the park I needed for my investigation. It opened right away, and I walked down the rows of plants, bushes, small trees, and flowers until I arrived at Kenny's office. I buzzed myself in and looked around. Everything was dark, and the computers were asleep.

I jiggled a mouse, and the screen lit up with the system used in the park. I had used the facilities services portal to order supplies, so I hoped the landscaping department was set up the same way. I noticed the options were different than what I was used to, but there was one called "Orders."

I sat at the desk, keeping an ear out for anyone who might barge in and be surprised to find me here. My fingers trembled as they gripped the mouse, navigating to the orders page, which was a gigantic spreadsheet. After finding the search bar, I typed in "*Atropa belladonna.*"

Nothing came up.

So I searched "Deadly nightshade."

Nothing.

Well, drat, this meant the order for those bushes didn't go through the park's ordering system at all. At least Kenny wasn't lying when he said he didn't order them. I figured that exonerated him, though he could have bought them himself and brought them in. I wondered how much something like that cost, so I went to the "place an order" page and typed it in again.

This time, I was redirected to a website for a huge wholesale plant warehouse. Several different results for *Atropa belladonna* appeared, everything from seeds to large, fully-grown plants. They weren't especially expensive. So, basically, anyone could get their hands on them.

I was still thinking of Ellie. She was a plants person—studying for a master's in horticulture. She had a reason to dislike Charlotte. Perhaps she wanted Walker back. Maybe she was only with Kenny so she could stay close to Charlotte and Walker. It all made sense to me. Plus, she'd had access to the park and knew her way around.

I shut down the computer and jumped back in the golf cart, driving around to a different building where props and set pieces were made for displays on rides and all over the park. I had never been in the set shop before, but I knew of it. I was surprised to hear machines whirring and buzzing and music almost loud enough to overpower the sounds when I let myself in with my master key card.

I stood there for a moment at the door, and then heads began to pop up from workstations like prairie dogs on alert. Every last buzz and whirring wound down. Then the music stopped, and silence filled the vast space as a dozen or more pairs of eyes just stared at me.

I raised my hands, palms up. "Hi. I'm Cat Lyon from Custodial. Who is in charge here? Can I talk to them for a sec?"

A husky-looking woman wearing a navy park polo shirt and coveralls took a pair of goggles off her eyes and headed toward me like a charging bull. Her hand jutted out when she reached me. "I'm Millie. Are you *the* Cat Lyon?"

Was that an accusation or more fangirling? "Um...I guess so?"

Her brusque tone softened. "The one responsible for saving the park? Keeping it open?"

"Yeah, I guess that's me." I shrugged. I'd never get used to having any degree of notoriety.

She slapped me on the back with a huge grin on her face. "Never thought I'd get to meet you. Well, come on back to my office. Can I get you something to drink? Water? Coffee? Soda?"

"Oh, no, I'm fine, but I'd love to talk to you for a second." I smiled as she led me down an aisle between workbenches where I could see some of the things the workers were building. It looked like they had shifted focus from fall and Halloween-themed pieces to Christmas themes. One piece looked destined to become a large wooden candy cane, while some wooden boxes of various sizes looked like maybe they would become Christmas gifts.

She gestured me inside a tiny cubicle in the corner of the room. It had huge windows overlooking the floor and was cramped with a metal desk and metal shelves holding binders like the ones I saw in Kenny's office. "This is a busy place," I observed, looking around the tight quarters. "I didn't realize you have a second shift too. We work at the same time."

She smiled. "Yes, it's twenty-four-seven work here in the set shop. We build pretty much every art and decorative piece in the park. The only thing we don't build in here are the individual ride components. That's done in the next building over. They do the tracks, cars, boats, and all the control stuff. Much more technical stuff over here. Our department is more like art."

"I can see that. It must be a lot of fun." I folded my hands in my lap as I tried to get a read on her. She seemed to have a very robust personality—booming voice, animated facial expressions.

"Yeah, we do have a good time here. We get to combine creativity with technical know-how. Not too many people get to do that."

"I know we don't in my department. Some of it might be technical know-how, but the rest is brute force." I laughed.

"Well, you get to solve murders too, as I understand it." She grinned at me, showing me a chipped front tooth. "Must be a nice break from cleaning."

"Oh, it is." I leaned forward. "I came here to ask you about the set you built for Mr. Carson's daughter's wedding."

"Oh, isn't it nifty? Mr. Carson brought his daughter and her fiancé in here over the summer, and we talked about their vision for their wedding day. We decided we could easily incorporate it with our Halloween décor this year. It took us a while to make all the pieces for it, but we just kept building and adding until it had just the vibe they wanted."

"Oh, yes, it's really cool. Were you guys going for a certain look? Did they give you any inspiration for it?"

"Yes, Charlotte and her wedding coordinator visited a few times and gave us photos from some of the famous church graveyards around Charleston. We tried to stay true to those historical grave markers—some of them are replicas of tombstones from St. Philips, St. Michael's, and the Circular Congregational Church," she explained.

"Oh, is there one for Harriet Mackie?" I asked.

Millie squinted and bit her lip while she thought about it. "Sorry, I'm not familiar with any individual stones. I just supervised the team making them. Is that one of the markers in the historic district?"

"Yes, ma'am," I explained, "it's the gravestone of a bride who was murdered right before her wedding in 1804."

Millie gasped. "Oh, well, that one might have been inappropriate. Hope the team didn't include her, but they might not have known."

Looking at her surprised expression, I tended to believe she wasn't familiar with the legend of the dead bride. "You said you had a team working on the project?"

She nodded. "Yes, a team of five. They do beautiful work. Some of the pieces were 3D-printed. Our tech person does those. Some were made out of fiberglass—we have an amazing fabricator who can make almost anything out of any material. Then we have a pair of artists who do the painting, and another designer who does floral and fabric and other soft goods."

"Sounds like an amazing team." I filled my lungs with air and let out a breath, trying to figure out how to pose my next question. I swallowed hard—I had to get this right, or she was going to clam up. "I noticed a couple of new gravestones there today. Do you know why they were added last-minute?"

Her dark brows furrowed. "Last minute? We've had all the grave markers made for two months, and they were all placed over a week ago. There shouldn't have been any new ones."

"So your team didn't design one with the bride's name, birth date and a death date for tomorrow on it?"

Millie leaped up from her chair. "Oh my gosh, what?! How did that happen?" She ran from the room, out onto the floor, and started screaming.

I couldn't understand her from inside the office, but it was clear she didn't know about the gravestones. That meant someone on the outside had placed them there. Just like someone on the outside must have brought in the belladonna plants. The gravestones showed up when Ellie arrived in town.

It was starting to look more and more like she was our "ghost."

Twenty

CATHERINE

I was hoping to run into Zoe on my way back to The Haunted Wood, but I didn't see my little furry friend anywhere. In fact, I hadn't seen her in a while—not since she brought me the book of poisons. I hadn't had a chance to ask her about the ghost or if they'd seen anyone matching Ellie's description.

Speaking of which…I was trying to figure out if Ellie looked like the "ghost" we'd seen a few nights ago. With the right makeup and lighting, I figured it was possible. How did she get into the park and set up without anyone knowing, though? How did security not see her on their cameras?

I had so many questions and not very many answers after visiting Kenny's office and the set shop. I was only fairly certain that a current employee of Fairytale Forest wasn't responsible for the craziness. Once I arrived back at the woods, it appeared they were rehearsing the ceremony a second time. I slid into a seat next to Gloria, who was tapping her foot impatiently on the ground as Marci droned on about entrance cues.

"Wow, she's quite bossy, isn't she?" I whispered in Gloria's ear.

"Yeah, we just had a five-minute break. Then she yelled 'Take five, everyone!' like a director on a set. I pulled Jocelyn aside and asked if she was always this way, and she said, yes, she has a theater background."

I laughed. "Well, that's pretty apparent, what with the theatrical dresses she's always wearing. It's like she's always in costume."

"Yes, but she is very organized, and I have no doubt things will go smoothly tomorrow after all this practice. The show must go on!" Gloria quipped, and we both stifled laughter as Marci looked over at us with a glare.

"I guess Jayden didn't make it?"

Gloria shook her head. "Not yet."

After we got another dirty look, this time from Charlotte herself, we decided to behave ourselves and sit quietly until the rehearsal was over. Then, finally, Marci seemed satisfied that everyone knew their places, lines and blocking.

"Thank you all for coming to the rehearsal tonight," Walker addressed the wedding party and spectators. "Please, everyone, join us at the Magical Mushroom for our rehearsal dinner!"

Ellie had arrived at some point while I was gone. She sidled up to Kenny, whispering something in his ear that I wished I could hear. Lip-reading was a skill I should learn for my side gig here as a sleuth. I wanted to talk to Gloria, but I also wanted to keep an eye on Ellie. Hmm…this was when I needed Zoe's help, and she was nowhere to be found.

Gloria tapped me on the shoulder. "So, what happened? Did you find out anything on your travels?"

"We should find a place to talk before heading over to the

rehearsal dinner. But I don't want to miss any of it, either. And I know Mr. Forest wants us there." I felt torn, needing to be in three places at once.

"What did you do with the golf cart? We can take our time getting over to the restaurant." Gloria smiled. "I believe everyone else is walking."

I nodded. "It's parked at the back gate."

"Oh, you went out to the greenhouse, did you?" She gave me a conspiratorial grin.

"And the set shop," I confirmed.

While everyone began to move en masse to the front of The Haunted Wood, we hightailed it to the back gate, where I'd left the golf cart. There was a single floodlight illuminating us as we sat in the golf cart in the dark, silent park.

"It's a little creepy out here, isn't it?" Gloria's eyes shifted around us, but it was hard to see anything past the light.

"You afraid the ghost is coming back?" I joked.

Gloria shuddered. "Well, she can't hurt us now, can she? You still think it's Ellie?"

"Well, the ghost was blonde, and she's blonde. I don't remember if she looked like Ellie, but I'm sure with lighting and makeup, it's possible."

"So what did you find out from your little field trip out back?" Gloria probed.

"I got into the ordering database for landscaping—no *Atropa belladonna* ordered. So someone must have brought it in."

"Unless it was ordered through a different system," Gloria argued.

"Well, that spreadsheet seemed to be every plant we've used in the park in the past year, so I doubt it. And I did look them up to see if you can just buy them easily, and it seems you can. They aren't especially expensive either. All the places selling them warn they are poisonous."

"Interesting. So, easy to come by. But she would have had to get them into the park with no one noticing," Gloria pointed out. "What happened at the set shop?"

I told her about meeting Millie and how surprised she was to hear about the two new gravestones. I mentioned that Millie said all the gravestones had been fabricated months ago.

"Okay, so what if it's not Ellie?" Gloria questioned. "Does anyone else make sense, have the access and the ability to get the plants, gravestones, place the locket, and pretend to be a ghost?"

"The ghost was…a real person, right?" My voice shook as I searched for the right words. The memory still gave me the heebie-jeebies. "I mean, as opposed to it being like…a projection and recording, right?"

"It was pretty foggy due to the rain," Gloria said. "Honestly, it was dark, foggy, and I was scared out of my mind. I think it could have been a projection. It really seemed to glow. But the white dress…it looked real, like it was blowing in the wind."

"I know… I'm so confused by everything! But, yes, let's go through a list really quick, and then we've got to get over to the restaurant just in case something happens. Ellie is there. What if she tries something with Charlotte in front of everyone?"

"Surely there are enough people around Charlotte that won't happen." Gloria sighed.

"Well, it happened to Harriet Mackie," I pointed out. "She must have been surrounded by people on her wedding day, probably other women…and she still got poisoned."

"You don't think Ellie would really try to hurt her, do you? Maybe this is all just a big joke. We already know Kenny is a big prankster. If she knows about the chess piece, maybe she just decided to ramp up the joke to a new level?" Gloria theorized.

"Maybe she and Kenny are working together? That's the only thing that makes sense. He has access to the parks." I got a mental image of him helping her stage the ghost scene. We spoke to him later that night, so he definitely could have been there. But was she?

"But he said he would never plant the poison berry bushes because of the cats. And he seemed pretty convicted about it," Gloria reminded me.

"But, again, who else could it be?" I went down a mental list of suspects. "It's not Jocelyn. It's not Walker's sister, Ruth. I don't know much about Brittany, but I don't think she has a motive like Ellie does. It's not Marci—she was pretty sure Kenny was involved, and she's the one who told us he was a prankster, not to mention that Ellie was Walker's ex-girl-friend. Plus, what kind of wedding coordinator sabotages their client's wedding? That can't be good for business."

"True, true. I wish Jayden had shown up with that library book," Gloria said. "If we could just get the name—it would clear a lot of stuff up."

"We better get over to the restaurant. I have a bad feeling about what might happen next…"

Gloria groaned. "I don't like it when you get a bad feel-ing." She looked up at the sky, where the clouds were thick-ening, and uttered something in Gullah. I didn't catch it this time.

ZOE

"Psst…psst! Zoe! Over here!" a voice called out from one of the bushes near the entrance of the park, not too far from Scar's territory.

The fur along my spine rose as I whipped around to see a pure-white form step into the light. When a striped tail whipped around the body, I knew it was Snow.

"What do you want, Traitor?" I sneered. "You know, I watched some historical documentary about how the bipeds fought for independence from a king. They too had a traitor in their midst. His name was Benedict Arnold. I think I'm gonna just start calling you that. Maybe Benny for short."

"Zoe, I know you're mad, but give me a chance to explain…" He reached out a paw to touch me. "Please?"

I jumped back at least two feet. "No way! I don't trust you as far as I can throw you, which isn't far because you're kinda a big tom."

"Please, I just want to say a few things. I need to get away from here though. Scar has all kinds of spies. I have to be careful." His head swiveled around as he appeared to be checking the shadows for lurking felines.

"Again, don't trust you. Not now, not ever. I was stupid to ever believe all those stupid lies you told me, acting like you were interested in me." I sharpened my claws on a nearby root.

"I was!" he insisted. "I still am. Please, Zoe, you have to listen."

I started to sashay away, holding my head high as my tail waved proudly. "Talk to the bootay, Benny."

He followed me. "C'mon, I know a safe place to talk. Follow me."

"I wouldn't follow you if you were the last feline on earth, Benny."

"Don't call me that."

"You're right," I scoffed. "I should call you something even more descriptive: like Mouse Turd or Scum of the Earth."

"Zoe, I want to help you," he pleaded. "Please let me. Look, I've already helped you, and you don't even know how…"

"I highly doubt that. You clearly only think of yourself. You're just a spoiled housecat." I picked up my pace, bounding over a puddle leftover from the earlier rain and landing solidly on all four paws.

"Scar wanted to ambush and attack you," he revealed.

I came to a screeching halt. We were nearing the pond, and I could smell the water. "He wanted to what?"

"He wanted to kill you. He was already furious over the stunts you pulled—and he blamed you for Klaus's death because he knows you're friendly with the bipeds, and he figured the bipeds put the plants there that made the mouse Klaus ate sick."

"Well, that's not what happened at all. My biped friend helped me figure out why the cats were getting sick so that nobody else got sick!"

Did I just call Cat my friend?

Well, I'd thought Snow was my friend, and look how that turned out.

"Zoe, he wanted to kill you, and I talked him into making you turn yourself in instead. And I came up with the 'ruin the wedding' thing and acted like it would be this huge deal that would really upset the bipeds and they wouldn't want anything to do with you again."

Hmmm.

That did explain a lot because I couldn't understand why Scar would care about some stupid biped ceremony.

"What was your plan for ruining it?"

Snow sat up straight, and his lips twisted into an almost-smile. "You know how bipeds are really uncomfortable by feline behinds?"

"Um…okay?" It was true, though. If I stuck my behind in a security biped's face, they always acted grossed out and swatted me away.

"Well," Snow emitted a smug purr, "we were planning on showing them our behinds during the event. Like over and over again. Relentlessly. Like *gratuitously.*"

I squinted as I surveyed him, appearing to be highly amused by this ridiculous plan. It had none of the nuance or finesse of the plans I had orchestrated to humiliate Scar and his thugs, and I didn't even understand how them executing it would reflect poorly on me.

But maybe he was banking on me giving myself up before that.

"You don't seem very impressed," Snow said.

"Um, no, as a matter of fact, I'm not." I twirled in a circle and sat down, curling my tail around myself. "There is a chance the wedding will be ruined, but it won't be by a cat. It will be by another biped. That is what my biped friends have been trying to figure out. Someone is harassing them and the biped getting married."

He shuddered at the M word, probably remembering my harrowing description of it earlier.

"So, why are you telling me this, anyway?"

He stepped closer to me. "Zoe, I was blackmailed into helping them. They threatened to expose me to The Wrangler, since I'm here unofficially. Your clowder has done a wonderful job accepting me, integrating me, and helping me assimilate, but the truth is, I'm not one of you. I've not been vetted…and I'm not sterilized."

"What?" Now his scent made more sense to me.

"Yeah…so Vinny kept telling me, if I didn't agree to help

them, I was going to get captured and the ol' snip-a-roo, if you know what I mean."

"Ew."

"Yeah, exactly."

"So how are you here now? Aren't they going to hunt you down and make good on their promise?"

He straightened up to his full height, looking tall and proud as he was silhouetted by the lights reflecting off the pond. "I figured it was worth the risk, because you help everyone, Zoe. You are a good cat, and you don't deserve to be deported. I figured if I got deported, it was only because I deserved to be. I'm not really one of you guys anyway."

I stepped closer to him, mesmerized by the way the lights painted his fur a shade of silver, reminding me of the locket I gave to Cat not that long ago. "Snow, if everything you just said is true—which is still a big if, as far as I'm concerned—then you're just as much 'one of us' as any other cat in the park."

He licked his lips. "Then let me prove it to you, Zoe. I have a plan."

Twenty-One

We pulled the golf cart up to the back entrance of the restaurant, trying to hide it from view. Then we climbed out and walked around to the front, about to make a dramatic late entrance, when we heard a shout from the pathway emerging from the stand of trees between the restaurant and the pond.

"Cat! Gloria, wait!" came a familiar voice, and seconds later, two figures appeared. "Wait, don't go in yet. We need to talk to you first."

It was Jayden and Nora, out of breath. They must have run all the way through the park. Jayden cleaned up nicely in a shirt and tie, and Nora was wearing a classy V-neck wrap dress with heels. She was a superhero for being able to keep up with Jayden on their run.

"What do you have for us?" I asked as they stopped to catch their breath.

Nora stepped forward, clutching her purse in one hand and a folded piece of paper in the other. "We got the circulation record for the book. It doesn't mean anything to us, but maybe it will help you?"

Gloria flashed me an excited look as I took the piece of paper from her and unfolded it. I scanned the record of checkouts for the book, my eyes landing on the last name on the list.

Folding it back up and sticking it in my pocket, I turned to Gloria. "We've got her."

Gloria let out an excited squeal, then held the door open as we all filed into the restaurant.

THE MAGICAL MUSHROOM RESTAURANT'S MAIN DINING AREA was designed to look like you're dining inside an enchanted forest. There were trees staggered between the tables, which looked to be carved from their trunks with cozy booths surrounding them. Clumps of moss decorated with mushrooms and little fairy toadstool houses appeared in random spots, and it looked as though fairies zoomed through the air, darting between trees and leaving trails of colorful sparkles in their wake.

The darkness and the crowd of people made it difficult for me to ascertain what was happening at first, but when we started walking the yellow-brick path between the trees, things became clear. There was a long table set up at the back that hosted the bride, groom, and their parents and siblings. The wedding party was at another table set up across from it, and the rest of the guests filled the cozy tree booths.

Gloria jerked on my sleeve when I started to veer toward the bride and groom's table. "Aren't we looking for Ellie? She's over there." She pointed to the wedding party's table.

I shook my head. "She's not our girl."

"What?" Gloria's incredulous wide eyes popped open as she tried to steer me off the path and into a private corner. But I saw our suspect wheeling a cart holding a teapot, a few tiny teacups, and matching saucers out of the back where the kitchen was. She rolled it right to Charlotte's side of the table and offered her one of the dainty cups.

When I saw the library circulation record for *Poisonous Plants of North America*, it all clicked into place.

Only one person had access to the wedding venue any time she wanted.

Only one person had connections to a local theater company.

Only one person had extensive knowledge of Harriet Mackie's death.

Only one person had a dramatic flair and raging jealousy of the bride.

Only one person had checked out a book on poisonous plants.

And she was about to serve the bride tea.

I lunged for the teacup just as Charlotte was lifting it to her mouth, knocking it out of her grasp. "Noooooo!!! Don't drink it!" I shouted, causing every single head in the restaurant to turn toward us. The low rumble of conversations abruptly stopped, and the only sound was the teacup crashing to the floor in a million pieces.

"What are you doing?" Marci shrieked, taking two steps back with the teapot still in her hands.

"Put down the teapot," I commanded. "Charlotte, I have reason to believe Marci poisoned your tea."

"What?!" Charlotte stood up, turning to face the one I'd just accused.

Marci's helpful, supportive wedding coordinator mask evaporated, revealing a face full of rage as her eyes and lips thinned and her nostrils flared. Her chest heaving with fury, she threw the pot of tea down toward the table, hot tea flying through the air causing utter pandemonium.

In the midst of the commotion, Marci fled out the back of the restaurant. I screamed to anyone who was listening, "Chase her down and call the police!"

Jayden, Nora and others with much younger legs took off after her. Marci was wearing those cute ivory suede boots—there was no way she was going to get far, especially in the mud.

Mr. Forest, Mr. Carson and their wives came rushing toward Charlotte, who had collapsed into one of the booths sobbing. She had burns from the tea on her arms and was waving them wildly as her parents settled in, one on each side of her.

Kenny and Ellie shouted, "We'll get some ice!" and headed into the kitchen. Jocelyn and her husband followed them.

Gloria and I stood there, taking in the chaotic scene, our hearts pounding. "How did you know?" Gloria asked, and I handed her the circulation printout Nora was able to nab for us.

She looked it over, shaking her head. "Marcella Beauchamp. I can't believe it."

"I think I know why she wanted to coordinate the wedding so bad, especially after she wasn't asked to be a bridesmaid. After her own engagement fell apart... To Marci, it always seemed like Charlotte Carson led a charmed life. Everyone loves her; she always had boyfriends and girl-friends; her dad was a bigwig at the local amusement park; she landed the eligible bachelor, Walker Buckley—oh, and Charlotte getting chosen for the sorority and not Marci didn't sit well either. I think she was just trying to get Char-lotte to call the wedding off—I hope she didn't really mean to take it this far."

"That makes sense. So how did you know it wasn't Ellie?" Mrs. Forest asked.

"Ellie worked here this summer, and she would have had access to the ordering and the set shop, but she didn't order the belladonna plants. Plus, I couldn't figure out how she would have gotten the locket into the park. She said she'd never heard of the ghost story before, and she didn't grow up in Charleston. I believed her."

Mr. Forest stepped back from the booth where he'd been talking to Charlotte and her parents and headed for us. "Good work, Catherine and Gloria. I guess all the tea is gone? We can't test it for poison?"

Sadly, he was right about that. "Let's go outside and see if they were able to catch her." I rubbed my hands together. This was going to be good. "I have a feeling we'll find evidence on her."

Mr. and Mrs. Carson climbed out of the booth. "We're going too."

The group that had dashed to the kitchen for ice appeared with several cold compresses, which Charlotte pressed to her arms before proclaiming, "I'm coming too," as she slid out of the booth. Her fiancé took her hand and helped her to her feet as she held the ice to her burns. "I have a few things I'd like to say to my so-called wedding coordinator."

When we stepped out into the cool fall air, the sound of police sirens carried on the breeze. We walked around to the back of the restaurant, taking the path through the wooded area toward the Wishing Pond.

Sure enough, in a heap just feet from the pond was a ball of orange tulle fanning out around a woman sitting in a puddle, mud caked all over her. Her blonde hair had come loose and hung around her face like a curtain as she sobbed. She was surrounded by Jayden, Nora, and the others, who were making sure she didn't get away before the police came to arrest her.

I calmly walked to her and picked up the leather portfolio she'd been using to coordinate the wedding. When I unzipped it, I reached into the back pocket and pulled out a sprig of black berries.

"*Atropa belladonna!*" Gloria gasped. "Now that I know what it is, I'd know it anywhere."

"You tried to poison Charlotte," I accused, causing the bride to gasp.

"No, I didn't! They're just pretty berries, and you can't prove anything was in that teapot." She started to brace herself so she could stand, but those mud-caked ivory suede boots could find no traction. She slipped and, with a comically loud splat, fell right back down into the mud.

Before any of us could say another word, a golf cart full of police sped onto the scene. Detective Shelly Towers, with whom I was well acquainted after helping her solve two murder mysteries, stepped out of the passenger side with a uniformed officer who had been driving.

"Evening, everyone. What seems to be going on here?"

Mr. Forest stepped forward, extending his hand. "I'm sorry to see you again under these circumstances, Detective Towers, but at least this time I think we prevented the murder."

"I wasn't trying to kill her!" Marci shouted.

"What *were* you trying to do?" I asked, noticing our detective friend had taken out her ubiquitous mini yellow legal pad to jot down notes.

This time Marci made it to her feet, her gaze bouncing from face to face in the crowd as she tried to smooth out her voluminous skirts that were caked with mud. "I wasn't trying to kill her. I just—" She sighed. "I was angry she didn't ask me to be a bridesmaid, and, well, I thought I'd have a little fun with her and Jocelyn, her matron of honor. So I decided to use the ghost story about Harriet Mackie to harass her a little bit. I hoped she'd be so scared, she'd call off the wedding!"

"Why were you targeting me and Gloria?" I asked. "You sent that bouquet to the Forests' beach house, and we were the ones staying there."

Marci huffed, "Well, I thought Charlotte and Jocelyn were there that weekend. I didn't know you and Gloria were going to be there."

Jocelyn's hand flew to her face. "We were supposed to have your bridal shower there that weekend!" she exclaimed, looking at Charlotte. "But we moved it to our house on King Street because Dad said the lovely ladies who had been helping him solve crimes in the park were going to be staying at the beach house that week."

"Yeah, the bridal shower I wasn't even invited to!" Marci cried.

"It was for her family, Marci, sheesh!" Jocelyn fired back. "We were only hosting it for them."

"So let me get this straight," Detective Towers stepped forward, "you were stalking and harassing Charlotte Carson, and then you tried to poison her?"

"I just put a little in her tea to make her sick—it wouldn't have killed her," Marci insisted. Then she realized she'd just admitted to poisoning the bride.

"Yeah, I need to take you in for further questioning." The detective, dressed in a no-frills charcoal-gray pantsuit, looked the suspect up and down. "Come along—that's quite the outfit you've got there."

There was a snicker from a few of the younger members of our audience as the uniformed officer took Marci Beauchamp by the arm and led her to the golf cart. "I don't think she's a flight risk in that dress and those boots," Detective Towers pointed out. She dipped her chin at me and

Gloria, then at Mr. Forest. "I'll be in touch for further statements. I understand there's a wedding here tomorrow?"

We all nodded and murmured in the affirmative.

"I'll work around that. Have a good evening, folks!" She gave a little wave before climbing into the golf cart next to Marci.

As soon as they drove away, Charlotte rushed toward us, flinging her arms around both Gloria and me. "Thank you, thank you, thank you so much for everything! You just prevented a disaster from happening on what's supposed to be the happiest day of my life."

Walker was right behind her, extending his hand for a shake, but he ended up in a big group hug with his betrothed, Gloria and me before Mr. and Mrs. Carson got in on the action. Then Jocelyn and Mr. and Mrs. Forest joined in too.

We went from crimefest to lovefest in about thirty seconds flat.

Twenty-Two

It had been a long night, and I had to hope the plans I put in motion would keep me out of trouble. I needed to know what to expect as far as the wedding was concerned, and there was only one way to get that information. I needed to speak with Cat.

I tracked her down outside the mushroom restaurant later in the evening. She was sitting on a bench with Gloria. Conveniently, no one else was around. Thinking it was safe to interact, I wandered out of the bushes and rubbed up against her leg.

"Oh!" she yelped, her hand flying to her chest. "Oh, Zoe! It's you, thank goodness. Y'all about gave me a heart attack."

I sat on my haunches, waiting for her to collect herself. When she looked ready to interact, I locked my eyes with hers. "How's it going?"

"It's going great now." She wiped her forehead dramatically. Her friend giggled when she did this.

"Is that sarcasm?" Cats were masters of sarcasm, but it

wasn't always easy for us to detect it in other species, particularly bipeds.

"You could say that. We finally figured out who was causing all the trouble around here—the person who poisoned the mice and made the cats who ate them sick," she clarified, smiling.

"Oh? Well, that's good news. I'm glad *someone's* drama is over." My tail twitched as I said the last few words.

"You know the term 'drama'?" Her eyebrow rose. "Was that sarcasm?"

I licked my lips. "I'm in the middle of something, but please, tell me about your day."

Judging by her response, she didn't seem to fully grasp my banter either: "It was the bride's wedding coordinator. She was jealous and vengeful."

"I only understood the second thing you said." I stretched out on the ground. It seemed like I might be here for a while.

"She planted the locket, the poisonous berries, pretended to be a ghost with the help of some makeup artists and set and lighting designers she knows from a local theater company, and even put on a white wedding gown to try to scare us away from investigating." Cat shook her head as she laughed at the apparent absurdity of it all.

"Wait, did you say white dress?" I cocked my head, my ears directed right at her.

"Yes, she pretended to be the ghost bride in the 'graveyard' where the wedding is going to be held tomorrow at dusk."

"The reason you two ran out of the graveyard in hysterics the other night?" I clarified.

"Yes! How did you know about that?" she asked.

"Because I am the one who got you help!" I tapped a paw on the ground. "Did you think The Wrangler just happened to stumble upon you?"

"Oh, I see. Well, thanks." She grinned and nudged Gloria. "Looks like Zoe is the one who called in the cavalry after we saw the ghost."

Gloria's hands flew to her face, covering up a gasp. "Oh my! Thank you so much, Zoe!"

I basked in their gratitude momentarily, and then it clicked. "Wait, you said she was wearing a white dress. Does she happen to have blonde hair too?" I remembered what one of the cats I interviewed said about carrying Mr. Cool Cat out in a basket.

"Indeed, she is a blonde," Cat revealed.

"Hmm…and where is this biped now?"

"Hopefully in jail," Cat said, sounding pleased with herself.

I hoped this criminal biped hadn't hurt Mr. Cool. "So… tell me about this…wedding tomorrow."

"It's slated for around the time the sun sets tomorrow. Slightly before that, all of the bride's and groom's family and friends will gather in some chairs set up in The Haunted Wood. Then there will be some music, and some people will walk down the aisle in between the chairs. There will be someone in charge who will perform some biped rituals, and then the bride and groom will be married and seal their promise to each other with a kiss."

"Gross."

She shrugged. "Well, that's the way we do it."

"Have you done this…wedding thing before, Cat?"

She smiled. "Oh, yes, I was dumb enough one time. When I was young. I'm a lot smarter now. I can't see ever making that kind of promise again."

"Yeah, I'm not going to pretend to understand what that's all about." My ears twitched as I got an itch right behind them and rushed to scratch it with my right front paw.

"So, all the bipeds will be gathered in the woods," I confirmed.

"That's right. Why, you planning to come watch?" she pondered.

"I just might." I licked my lips again. "Gotta see what this whole wedding thing is about. You bipeds sure are weird."

She smiled. "We sure are."

WE HEARD THE STEADY STREAM OF BIPEDS MAKING THEIR WAY through the park to enter the gates where the wedding was happening, and if the position of the sun was any indication, it would begin soon. Nervously looking over my shoulder as I made my way to the woods, I spotted my clowder behind me: Moony, Snow, Ice, Ziti, Amber, Daisy, Princess and Sass. Even Hank had pried his loaflike body off the ground and was almost keeping pace with the others.

"No matter what happens," Snow said, catching up with me, "we've got your back."

"Do you?" I still wasn't sure if I could trust him.

"If he betrays you again, Sis, I'm taking him down." Moony stopped his march long enough to hold up a paw and extend his nails like tiny switchblades. "It's lights out for you if you don't stay one hundred percent loyal to our clowder," he warned with a menacing sneer.

I ignored him and focused on the task at hand. "C'mon, let's go stop Scar from ruining this wedding."

Scar had, what, eight or ten goons besides himself? I might have had a similar number, but with any luck, we may get a little help.

"This is it, Zoe," Ziti said as we reached the open gate.

In the bushes that lined the fence on either side of the

gate, dozens of glowing eyes shone in the burgeoning darkness. My heart started to pound. Had Scar recruited the others? Had they forsaken me?

"Come out and show your faces," Amber shouted toward the bushes.

I braced myself, preparing to do battle with Scar, Vinny, and his thugs. The fur on my back, from my neck to my tail, spiked high as fear raced through me. I sharpened my claws on the ground, just waiting to see their ugly mugs emerge from the thick briars.

But that wasn't what happened at all.

First Delta stepped out, along with her fellow River Cats. Then the Night Ninjas appeared. Then another clowder. One by one, the cats emerged, standing steadfastly with me and against the evil of the Mafia Cats.

Delta, who was never one to waste words, addressed me in front of the crowd: "Zoe, you've always done your best to ensure safety and freedom for every single cat in this park. You've risked life and limb to make this place better for all of us, and we're here to express our solidarity with you and your clowder."

Cats don't cry or get overly emotional like those silly bipeds do, but something like pride welled up inside me. I wasn't sure if I deserved this kind of unwavering sacrifice and support, but I was happy to take it—along with another W against the scourge that was Scar and his ilk.

"Now, you go inside and watch your biped friends' wedding," Ziti said. "Take Snow and Moony with you. And we're gonna stand guard out here."

I hesitated, my grateful gaze bouncing along the line of felines stretching as far as the fence line did toward the horizon.

But Ice said, "Go ahead, Z! You deserve it!"

Music began to swell from big black boxes perched just

inside the gate, and it looked like the event might be underway. So, I looked at my two companions, and they both happily nodded, flanking me as I strutted through the gates, looking for an out-of-the-way place to watch. Moony guided us to some decorated bushes, and the three of us stretched out, making ourselves comfortable as pairs of bipeds began to walk down the aisle created by the two groups of chairs.

I spotted Cat and Gloria sitting in two chairs near the back and wished I could go sit with them, but I knew that wouldn't be prudent. It would almost be like giving Scar his way—likely getting me kicked out of the park.

The crowd began to make exaggerated "aww" sounds, drawing my attention to a biped male and female pushing a little cart decorated with lights and greenery. Perched in the middle of an enormous velvet pillow in the middle was…

Wait for it…

Mr. Cool Cat.

Right next to him was a smaller pillow with something tied on a string—something round and glittering.

I heard Cat gasp. "Oh my gosh—that's Zoe's missing cat friend. He's the ring bearer!"

I didn't know what a ring bearer was, but seeing my friend alive caused a flood of relief to surge through me. Moony laid one of his paws on top of mine and shot me a knowing look. I didn't know why Cool was taken, but it looked like he had been treated well. He was snoozing away until the loud bipeds caused him to jerk his chin up and look around.

His mouth opened, and his tongue lolled out as he closed his eyes again and went right back to sleep.

Apparently he'd found the *purrfect* retirement job.

CATHERINE

The wedding went off without a hitch, and the bride looked absolutely radiant. Everyone cheered when Walker and Charlotte sealed their vows with a kiss, then the recessional began to Michael Jackson's "Thriller," which I thought was a strange choice but completely on-brand for this unconventional Halloween-themed wedding. The wedding party even stopped in the aisle and started doing the zombie dance from the music video.

We were all riveted, clapping along as the bride and groom danced their wedding party out of the woods and into waiting golf carts that would take them to the reception area that had been set up in the Princess and the Pea castle. Jocelyn even pushed Zoe's friend Mr. Cool Cat in his special stroller, completely oblivious to the hubbub around him.

We waited for everyone to clear out, then went over to talk to Zoe and her friends. She sat up and yawned. "So, that was a wedding, huh?"

"Yup. What did you think?"

"Well, seeing Mr. Cool Cat alive and well was clearly the best part," she commented. "How in the world did he end up with those bipeds?"

I smiled—I'd heard this story earlier today. "Apparently, Marci took him one night when she was here. A few employees saw her carrying him out in a basket, but she told them Sam gave her permission, and no one even questioned her. After she was arrested, Kenny remembered one of his employees saying something about stealing the cat, so Jocelyn went over to her place to pick him up. They were going to return him to the park, but he seemed really comfortable at Mark and Jocelyn's house, so her dad said to keep him. He's an older guy, right?"

"Yes," Zoe confirmed. "Well, I'm glad he's getting a happy ending."

"Just like Walker and Charlotte," I agreed. "But it might not have been so happy without all your help. I don't know what Gloria and I would have done without you."

"Well," Zoe said, "cats are usually pretty solitary creatures, but if there's one thing I've learned during these past three crises here in the park, it's that helping each other out usually leads to success."

"That's a very pragmatic way of looking at it." I reached out my hand toward her.

She immediately balked at it. "What's that for?"

"It's a biped tradition—shaking hands. It's done as a way of agreeing to a deal or as a greeting. It's basically done out of friendship and goodwill."

She tapped her paw to my hand. "I guess I can get behind that."

WE MANAGED TO ARRIVE AT THE RECEPTION JUST AS THE BEST man and matron of honor were giving the toasts. Kenny's toast was full of inside jokes and not-so-gentle ribbing—not surprising considering his jokester reputation, but Jocelyn's toast was quite a bit more poignant.

"Charlotte has been my very best friend since we were babies, thanks to our dads working together here at Fairytale Forest," she began. "We spent every summer here, riding the rides and later working in the park. This place shaped who we both are today, and I'd like to think it made us into strong, brave, resilient women. Charlotte faced a pretty big threat in the lead-up to her special day with Walker, and if it wasn't for two other brave, strong, resilient women, this day could have had a very different outcome. So, I want to take a moment to thank Catherine Lyon and Gloria Bress for all their help."

Everyone took a moment to stand and applaud Gloria and me. Mr. and Mrs. Forest were clapping the loudest, or maybe it just seemed that way since we'd been invited to sit with them at their table. To think we'd gone from often overlooked custodians to two of the most important members of the Forests' incredible team was mind-blowing.

But I wouldn't have it any other way.

Gloria turned to me with a smile, resting her hand on mine, much like Zoe had done earlier. "Well, what do you think our next adventure will be?"

I cocked my head and let a sly smile curl the corners of my lips. "I don't know, but as long as we face it together, I know it'll be a fun one."

THE END

Follow the Cat, Gloria, and Zoe's adventures here: Felines of Fairytale Forest

Join my newsletter for updates, giveaways and more! Bit.ly/ KLMontgomerynews

About the Author

K.L. Montgomery writes sweet romance, romcom, and cozy mystery with heroines like her: with extra curves and life experience. A librarian in a former life, she now also works as an editor and runs the 6000-member Indie Author Support group on Facebook in addition to publishing under two names.

Though she remains a Hoosier at heart, K.L. shares her coastal Delaware home with some furry creatures and her husband, a real-life detective, who is on the furry side as well. She has an undying love for her three sons, Broadway musicals, the beach, Seinfeld, the color teal, IU basketball, paisleys, and dark chocolate.

facebook.com/KLsBeachBunnies

instagram.com/k.l.montgomery

bookbub.com/authors/k-l-montgomery

tiktok.com/@klmontgomeryauthor

amazon.com/stores/K.L.-Montgomery/author/B00V2IEEUQ

Also by K.L. Montgomery

Felines of Fairytale Forest

Murder by Moonlight

Death in the Dark

Spirits after Sunset

Dangerous Curves Series

Betrayal at the Beach

Mystery at the Marina

Shooting at the Shore

Poisoned at the Pier

Bribery on the Boardwalk

Homicide at High Tide

Mischief Under the Mistletoe

Panic at the Playhouse

Con Artist on the Coast

Music Murder Mystery Series

The Sound of Murder

West Side Murder

Little Shop of Murder

Once Upon a Murder

Romance in Rehoboth Series (romantic comedy)

Music Man

The Flip

Plot Twist

Badge Bunny

Wedding War

Stage Mom

Shark Bite

Contemporary Romance Standalones

Given to Fly

The Light at Dawn

Reconstructed Heart

Women's Fiction

Fat Girl

Green Castles

Nonfiction

The Fat Girl's Guide to Loving Your Body

www.ingramcontent.com/pod-product-compliance
Lightning Source LLC
Chambersburg PA
CBHW061809190726
48289CB00007B/2127